The Next Person
You Meet in Heaven

Also by Mitch Albom

TUESDAYS WITH MORRIE

THE FIVE PEOPLE YOU MEET IN HEAVEN

HAVE A LITTLE FAITH

FOR ONE MORE DAY

THE TIME KEEPER

THE FIRST PHONE CALL FROM HEAVEN

THE MAGIC STRINGS OF FRANKIE PRESTO

FINDING CHIKA

The Next Person You Meet in Heaven

The Sequel to *The Five People You Meet in Heaven*

Mitch Albom

HARPER

An Imprint of HarperCollinsPublishers

First Harper mass market printing: March 2021
First Harper paperback printing: October 2019
First Harper hardcover printing: October 2018

Print Edition ISBN: 978-0-06-306355-6
Digital Edition ISBN: 978-0-06-229446-3

Cover design by Milan Bozic
Cover illustration © LEOcrafts/iStock/Getty Images

21 22 23 24 25 CPI 10 9 8 7 6 5 4 3 2 1

For Chika, the "little girl" of our lives,
who is already brightening heaven

And for all the nurses out there
who, like those who cared for Chika,
touch our souls more than they know

Note from the Author

This story, like *The Five People You Meet in Heaven*, was inspired by my beloved uncle, Eddie Beitchman, a World War II vet who thought he was "a nobody, who never did nothing."

When I was a child, Eddie told me of a night he nearly died at a hospital, and rose from his body to see his departed loved ones waiting for him, at the edge of the bed.

From that moment, I viewed heaven as a place where we encounter those we touched on earth, and where we get to see them again. But I recognize this is my view only. There are many others, along with many religious definitions, and all should be respected.

So this novel, and its version of the afterlife, is a wish, not a dogma, a desire that loved ones like Eddie find the peace that eluded them on earth, and realize how much we all affect one another, every day of this precious life.

The End

This is a story about a woman named Annie, and it begins at the end, with Annie falling from the sky. Because she was young, Annie never thought about endings. She never thought about heaven. But all endings are also beginnings.

And heaven is always thinking about us.

At the time of her death, Annie was tall and lean, with long curls of butterscotch hair, knobby elbows and shoulders, and skin that reddened around her neck when she was embarrassed. She had flashing eyes of a light olive shade, and a soft, oval face that coworkers described as "pretty once you get to know her."

As a nurse, Annie wore blue scrubs and gray running shoes to her job at a nearby hospital. And it was at that hospital where she would leave this world—after a dramatic and tragic accident—one month shy of her thirty-first birthday.

You might say that is "too young" to die. But what is too young for a life? As a child, Annie had been spared from death once, in another accident at a place called Ruby Pier, an amusement park by a great gray ocean. Some said her survival was "a miracle."

So perhaps she was older than she was meant to be.

"We are gathered here today . . ."

If you knew you were about to die, how would you spend your final hours? Annie, who did not know, spent hers getting married.

Her fiancé's name was Paulo. He had pale blue eyes, the color of shallow pool water, and a thick mop of raisin-black hair. She had met him back in grade school, during a game of leapfrog on an asphalt playground. Annie was a new student, shy and withdrawn. As she tucked her head, she repeated to herself, *I wish I could disappear.*

Then a boy's hands pushed down on her shoulders, and he landed in front of her like a dropped package.

"Hi, I'm Paulo," he said, smiling, a forelock falling over his brow.

And suddenly, Annie didn't want to go anywhere.

"Do you, Annie, take this man . . ."

With fourteen hours left to live, Annie took her wedding vows. She and Paulo stood beneath a canopy by a blueberry lake. They had lost touch as teenagers, and only recently had reunited. The years between were hard for Annie. She endured bad relationships. She suffered much loss. She came to believe she would never love a man again, and certainly never marry.

But here they were. Annie and Paulo. They nodded at the pastor. They took each other's hands. Annie wore white and Paulo wore black and their skin was tanned from hours in the sun. As she turned to face her future husband, Annie glanced at a hot air balloon floating above the sunset. *How lovely*, she thought.

Then she focused in on Paulo's grin, as wide as the horizon. There was nervous laughter as he struggled to get the ring on. When Annie held her finger up, everyone yelled, "Congratulations!"

Thirteen hours left to live. They walked down the aisle, arm in arm, a newly married couple with all the time in the world. As Annie brushed away her tears, she saw an old man in the last row, wearing a linen cap and a jut-jawed grin. Annie felt as if she knew him.

"Paulo," she whispered, "who is that man—"

But someone interrupted, "You look *so* beautiful!"— a teenaged cousin with braces on her teeth—and Annie smiled and silently mouthed, "Thank you."

When she looked back, the old man was gone.

Twelve hours left. Annie and Paulo took the dance floor, beneath strings of white bulbs. Paulo raised an arm and said, "Ready?" and Annie remembered a night in a junior high school gymnasium, when she marched up to Paulo and said, "You're the only boy who talks to me, so tell me right now if you will dance with me, yes or no, because otherwise I'm gonna go home and watch TV."

He'd smiled at her then as he smiled at her now, and they connected once again like puzzle pieces. A photographer jumped in and yelled, "Look here, happy couple!" and Annie instinctively hid her slightly smaller left hand behind Paulo's back, the hand that still bore scars from the accident more than twenty years ago.

"Beautiful," the photographer said.

Eleven hours left. Annie leaned on Paulo's arm and glanced around the ballroom. The celebration was winding down. Pieces of cake were half eaten, and women's high-heeled shoes were kicked off under the tables. It was a small affair—Annie didn't have much family—and she had chatted with nearly all the guests, many of whom had gushed, "Let's see each other more often!"

Paulo turned to Annie and said, "Hey, I made you something." Annie smiled. He was always making her little gifts. Wooden figures. Trinkets. He had learned to carve and paint in Italy, where his family moved when he was a teen. Back then, Annie thought she would never see Paulo again. But years later, on her nursing job, she walked past a hospital wing that was under construction, and there he was, working as a carpenter.

"Hey, I know you," he said. "You're Annie!"

Ten months later, they were engaged.

Annie was happy at first. But as the wedding approached, she grew anxious. She began losing sleep. "Whenever I plan things, they don't work out," she told Paulo. He put his arm around her shoulders and reminded her that she didn't "plan" to bump into him that day at the hospital, right?

Annie raised her eyebrows. "How do you know?"

Paulo laughed. "There's the Annie I'm gonna marry!"

But her worry remained.

"Here," Paulo said now, handing her a small, yellow, wiry creation, soft and fuzzy, with oval ears on top and oval feet on bottom.

"A rabbit?" Annie said.

"Uh-huh."

"From pipe cleaners?"

"Yeah."

"Where did you get this?"

"I made it. Why?"

Annie shifted on her feet, feeling suddenly uncomfortable. She looked across the floor and saw the old man from before. His chin was thick with salty whiskers and his suit was outdated by thirty years. But his skin was what drew Annie's attention; it was strange, almost radiant.

How do I know this man?

"Don't you like it?"

Annie blinked. "What?"

"Your rabbit."

"Oh. I love it. I do."

"I do," Paulo repeated, as if mulling it over. "We're saying 'I do' a lot today."

Annie smiled and rubbed the small creation. But something cold shot through her body.

A pipe cleaner rabbit—like the one Paulo just gave her—had been in Annie's hands the day of the fateful accident, a gift from the whiskered old man she was seeing now at her wedding.

A man who died more than twenty years ago.

His name was Eddie. He had worked at Ruby Pier. His job was fixing rides. Every day he greased the tracks and tightened the bolts and walked the park looking and listening for trouble. He kept pipe cleaners in his work shirt pocket to twist into toy figures for the younger customers.

The day of the accident, Annie had been left alone by her mother, who'd gone off with her latest boyfriend. Eddie was gazing at the ocean when Annie approached, wearing cutoff shorts and a lime green T-shirt with a cartoon duck on the front.

"'Scuuuse me, Eddie Maint'nance?" she said, reading the patch on his shirt.

"Just Eddie," he sighed.

"Eddie?"

"Hmm?"

"Can you make me . . . ?"

She put her hands together as if praying.

"C'mon, kiddo. I don't have all day."

"Can you make me an animal? *Can you?*"

Eddie looked up playfully, as if he had to think about it. Then he took out his yellow pipe cleaners and made her a rabbit—exactly like the one Paulo had just handed her.

"Thaaaank you," she said, dancing away.

Twelve minutes later, Eddie was dead.

⁂

The fatal incident occurred when a cart came loose from a tower drop ride called Freddy's Free Fall, two hundred feet above the ground. The cart dangled like a dying leaf as riders were pulled to safety. Eddie, watching from below, realized a cable was somehow fraying. If it snapped, the cart would plummet.

"GET BACK!" he screamed.

The crowd below scattered.

But Annie, in the confusion, ran in the wrong direction. She cowered at the ride's base, too frightened to budge. The cable broke. The cart dropped. It would have crushed Annie had Eddie not dived across the platform at the last instant and shoved her out of the way. Instead, the cart landed on Eddie.

It took his life.

But it took a piece of Annie as well. Her left hand. A chunk of metal broke loose upon impact and severed that hand cleanly from the bone. Some quick-thinking workers put the bloody appendage on ice, and paramedics raced Annie to the hospital, where surgeons worked for hours to repair the tendons, nerves, and arteries, grafting skin and using plates and screws to join the hand and wrist back together.

The accident made news around the state. Journalists labeled Annie "The Little Miracle of Ruby Pier." Strangers prayed for her. Some even sought an encounter, as if, through being saved, she held a secret to immortality.

But Annie, only eight years old, remembered nothing. The shock of the events wiped her memory clean, like a flame extinguished by a strong wind. To this day, she recalled only images and flashes and a foggy sense of being carefree the day she went to Ruby Pier and being something else when she returned home. The doctors used words like *conscious repression* and *traumatic disorder*, not knowing that certain memories are for this world and certain ones only come through in the next.

But a life had been exchanged for a life.

And heaven is always watching.

"Good luck! . . . God bless!"

Annie and Paulo scampered to the waiting limousine, ducking rice being thrown from paper cups. Paulo opened the door and Annie tucked inside, her dress trailing.

"Whoo-hoo!" Paulo laughed, sliding next to her.

The driver turned around. He was mustached, with brown eyes and teeth stained from tobacco.

"Congratulations, folks."

"Thank you!" they answered in unison.

Annie heard a rap on the glass; her Uncle Dennis was gazing down, a cigar in his mouth.

"All right, you two," he said, as Annie lowered the window. "Be good. Be careful. Be happy."

"Can't do all three," Paulo said.

Dennis laughed. "Then just be happy."

He grabbed Annie's fingers and she felt her eyes moisten. Dennis was her mother's brother and a respected surgeon at the hospital where Annie worked. After Paulo, he was Annie's favorite man in the world. Bald and paunchy and prone to easy laughter, Dennis had always felt more like a father to Annie than her real father, whose name was Jerry ("Jerry the Jerk," her mother called him) and who left when Annie was young.

"Thank you, Uncle Dennis."

"For what?"

"Everything."

"Your mom would have loved this."

"I know."

"She's watching."

"You think so?"

"Yep." He smiled. "Annie. You're married."

"I'm married."

He tapped her head lightly.
"A new life, kid."
Ten hours left.

No story sits by itself. Our lives connect like threads on a loom, interwoven in ways we never realize.

At the same time Annie and Paulo had been dancing at their wedding, forty miles away, a man named Tolbert went to grab his keys. He remembered that his truck was low on gas, and knowing it would be hard to find a station open at this hour, he grabbed the keys to his wife's car instead, a small, boxy vehicle with a tire low on air. He left the house without locking the door and glanced up at the clouds, which laced the moon in gray.

Had he taken the truck, this story would be different. Had Annie and Paulo not stopped for a final round of photographs, this story would be different. Had the limousine driver remembered to bring a bag that was sitting by his apartment door, this story would be different. The tale of your life is written second by second, as shifting as the flip of a pencil to an eraser.

"But we're gonna get maaaaa-rried!" Paulo sang, and Annie laughed as he forgot the words. She turned her back and pulled his strong grip over her. There are touches in your life that identify the person making contact, even if your eyes are closed. For Annie, it was Paulo's hands on her shoulders, as they were years ago in that leapfrog game.

As they were right now.

Annie saw his gold wedding band. She breathed a deep, contented sigh. They'd made it. They were married. She could stop worrying that something unexpected might derail things.

"I'm really happy," she said.

"Me, too," Paulo replied.

The limo pulled away. Through the window, Annie waved, as the guests clapped and gave the thumbs-up sign. The last person she saw was the old man in the linen cap, waving back, almost mechanically.

You have heard the phrase "heaven on earth." It suggests something wonderful, like the happy send-off from a wedding. But "heaven on earth" can mean something else; something that was happening to Annie right now, as the old man—Eddie from Ruby Pier—waved goodbye from the crowd.

At certain moments, when death is close, the veils pull back between this world and the next. Heaven and earth overlay. When they do, it is possible to glimpse certain souls already departed.

You can see them awaiting your arrival.

And they can see you coming.

Nine hours left. The night was misty and rain began to fall. The driver flipped on his windshield wipers. As they slapped back and forth, Annie thought about what lay ahead. First, their honeymoon, a long-planned trip to Alaska to see the northern lights. Paulo was obsessed with them. He'd shown Annie hundreds of photographs, and teasingly tested her on their origin.

"I know, I know," Annie would recite from memory. "Particles fly off the sun and blow to earth. They take two days to reach us. They break into our atmosphere where it's most vulnerable, at—"

"The top of the world," Paulo would finish.

"The top of the world."

"Very good," he'd declare. "You pass."

After Alaska, a new life awaited. Paulo and Annie had joined an organization that brought water to impoverished villages. They'd signed up for a year.

It was a big leap for Annie, who had never been out of the country. But her nursing skills could be put to good use, and Paulo believed in charity, often building things for free (his friends joked that he was "trying to win a merit badge every day of his life"). That made Annie smile. She'd made bad choices in men before. But Paulo. Finally. A partner to be proud of.

"I can't wait," Annie said, "to get to—"

The limo swerved and missed their exit.

"Dang," the driver said, looking in the rearview mirror. "The guy wouldn't let me in."

"It's all right," Paulo said.

"I'll get the next one—"

"That's fine—"

"Normally, I have my GPS—"

"It doesn't—"

"But I left it at home—"

"Don't worry—"

"That guy came up so fast—"

"It's OK," Paulo said, squeezing Annie's fingers. "We're enjoying the ride."

He smiled at his bride and she smiled back, with no idea of how the world had just changed.

∽

As the limo made its turn, heading back onto the highway, Annie noticed, through the rain, flashing taillights up ahead. A small, boxy vehicle was pulled over on the shoulder, and a man was crouched beside it, soaking wet. As the limo approached, the stranger stood and waved.

"We should stop," Annie said.

"Really?" Paulo said.

"He's drenched. He needs help."

"He'll probably be fine—"

"Sir, can you pull over?"

The driver eased in front of the stalled car. Annie looked at Paulo. "We can start our marriage with an act of kindness," she said.

"For good luck," Paulo said.

"Right," Annie said, although she was tempted to add she thought their marriage was already good luck.

Paulo pushed the door open. Rain drummed the pavement. "Hey, buddy!" Paulo hollered. "Trouble?"

The man nodded as Paulo approached. "My wife's car," he yelled. "The tire's flat. And of course she doesn't have a jack in the trunk. Do you have one?"

"A wife?"

"A jack."

"I'm kidding."

"Oh."

Rain ran down both their faces.

"I bet the limo has one."

"That'd be great."

"Gimme a second."

Paulo darted to the trunk of the limousine, smiling at Annie and making exaggerated arm motions, like a movie actor running in slow motion. The driver hit a button, the trunk opened, Paulo found the jack, and ran back to the stranded motorist.

"Thanks a lot," the man said. "Wives, you know?"

"Well, I'm not an expert," Paulo said.

Eight hours left. Annie watched through the rear window as Paulo and Tolbert wiped their palms on a rag. The tire had been changed. They chatted in the rain.

Annie fingered her wedding ring. She saw the men laugh. Paulo, standing closest to the highway, turned towards Annie and raised the stranger's wrist, as if signaling they were champions. For a moment, she felt amazed at her good fortune: a new husband in a wet tuxedo, so handsome he nearly glowed.

And then she realized the glow was from headlights. A car was coming up fast behind Paulo, illuminating his silhouette. Annie felt a rush of panic. She yelled his name. But Tolbert grabbed Paulo's arm and yanked him aside.

The car zoomed past.

Annie slumped in her seat.

"Hey, look at this," Paulo said, sliding in all wet beside her and holding up a business card. "The guy runs hot air balloons—"

Annie grabbed him. "Oh, my God!" she gushed, between kissing his wet cheeks and his wet hair and forehead. "I thought that car was going to hit you."

"Yeah, he was going fast. Good thing that guy—" Paulo saw her relief and took her face in his hands. "Hey. Annie. Hey." He squinted as if peering deep inside her. "I'm fine. No big deal. Nothing's gonna happen to me. We just got *married*."

Tears filled Annie's eyes.

"Let's get to the hotel," she whispered.

"To the hotel!" Paulo announced.

The driver pulled away.

Do you know what causes wind? High pressure meeting low pressure. Warm meeting cold. Change.

Change causes wind. And the bigger the change, the stronger the wind blows.

Life is much the same. One change blows in another. After the flat tire, the balloonist named Tolbert, concerned about driving on a spare, changed his plans and went home instead of to work, as he normally did this early on weekends. He called his assistant pilot and said, "Handle things until noon, OK?"

That assistant, a bearded young man named Teddy, changed his plans as he groggily replied, "No problem." He made coffee and got dressed.

Annie and Paulo, having shed their wedding clothes and shared a bed for the first time as a married couple, changed their plans as the sun began its rise through their hotel curtains. Annie stroked Paulo's hair as Paulo pushed into the pillow.

"Oh, man, I am beat!"

But Annie did not want things to end.

"If we don't go to sleep, technically it's still our wedding night, right?"

"I guess."

"In that case . . ."

She leaned over him and swiped a business card off the nightstand.

"A balloon ride!" Annie said.

"Noooo—"

"Yessss—"

"No-no-no—"

"Yes-yes-yes—"

"Annie—so impetuous!"

"I know. It's not like me. But I saw a balloon as we were saying our vows. Maybe it was a sign. The card says 'sunrise trips.'"

"Yeah, but—"

"Pleeeease . . ."

"Ohh . . . kay." Paulo squeezed his eyes shut, then popped them open. "Yes!"

Annie grabbed the phone. Her last call before dying began with, "Hi, are you flying today?"

Five hours left. Wearing light jackets against the morning chill, Annie and Paulo held hands near a large passenger basket in the middle of a grassy field. It all seemed so serendipitous: a business card, a phone call, a pilot named Teddy, a launching spot not far from their hotel. *What a wonderful future story to tell*, Annie thought. *A wedding night that ended in the clouds.*

A small crew ran propane burners to heat the air inside the balloon. Within minutes, it began to rise, like a yawning giant waking from its sleep. As the envelope filled to a massive pear-like form, Annie and Paulo leaned easily into each other, marveling at this silent airship that would lift them to the skies.

At that moment, they could not have known certain things: that Teddy was only a novice pilot, eager to prove himself; that he had agreed to take them up, despite a less-than-perfect weather report, because they were newlyweds; that newlyweds were a lucrative type of customer in the balloon world; that Teddy figured if these newlyweds told other newlyweds, it could be good for business.

And good for business was good for him.

"Ready to depart?" Teddy said.

He ushered Annie and Paulo into the basket. He shut the door behind them and, with the cables detached, let loose a stream of fire from the burner.

The balloon lifted from the ground.

"Oh, my God," Annie marveled forty minutes later, as they glided over vast, empty pastures. "This is unbelievable."

Paulo gripped the basket railing. "Why do people say 'unbelievable' about something that just happened? Wouldn't that make it believable?"

Annie grinned. "OK, genius."

"I'm just saying—"

A sudden gust hit the balloon, veering it sharply westward.

"Whoa," said Teddy.

"Whoa?" said Paulo.

"It's nothing," Teddy answered, eyeing the clouds. "Winds are kicking up. I'm gonna take it down a bit."

He pulled a valve, cutting the hot air, causing them to descend. A few minutes later, with the skies darkening, another strong gust pushed them farther west. Annie noticed they were getting closer to a thicket of trees.

"Can a person technically steer a balloon?" Paulo asked. "I'm not being critical or anything—"

"Just up and down," Teddy said, his hand on the propane burner. "We're fine. Don't worry."

They continued drifting in a westward direction. The winds increased. The clouds thickened. Teddy opened a hatch, allowing hot air to escape and the balloon to go even lower, hoping to avoid the gusts. A more experienced pilot would know that doing this could increase the risk of collision with the tree-tops, and staying high might be the safer, if rockier, course of action. But the more experienced pilot was

Tolbert, who, at that moment, was at an auto repair shop, getting a new tire.

Suddenly the trees were very close. "It's all right, no biggie," Teddy said, "but you might want to get down, in case we scrape a branch."

Then, as the woods drew closer, his voice intensified. "OK, get down!"

Annie and Paulo dropped inside the basket. The bottom half of the balloon smacked into high branches and the passengers were jolted to the side.

"Stay down!" Teddy yelled again. "I'm gonna land us!" He pulled the hatch even more, which caused a loud hissing sound. Looking up from her crouch, Annie glimpsed something dark and horizontal through the thick display of leaves.

Power lines.

The balloon made contact and pushed one line into another. Annie heard a sizzle. She saw a blinding flash. Sparks exploded and Teddy's knees buckled. He hollered, "Jesus!" and the basket dropped rapidly. Annie yelled and Paulo yelled and then everything was flipping and Annie couldn't get a straight view, trees, sky, floor, an arm, a rope, sky, shoes, fire.

They blew sideways and the basket smacked the earth, tossing the three passengers across its bottom. Annie saw flames, sky, ropes, Paulo, her elbow, blue jeans, sky, then Teddy disappeared over the side rail and the balloon began to lift again, hot air from the propane fire causing it to rise.

Suddenly, she felt Paulo's arms hard around her ribs. "Jump, Annie!" he yelled. She saw his face for an instant, but before she could say his name, he threw her from the basket and she was falling in the air, falling and then—*bang!*—she hit the ground, back first.

Her vision turned to stars, a million tiny lights blocking out the sun. When she finally refocused, she watched in horror as the balloon exploded in flames, and a figure dropped towards her, growing larger as it descended, arms flailing wildly.

Then Paulo, her new husband, thudded to earth.

Annie screamed.

In the dizzying hour that followed, one sentence clung to her like an anchor: *This is my fault.* Through the ambulance, the sirens, the gurney, the medics, the hospital, the emergency room, the doors that flew apart with a slam of a metal panel, that sentence would not let her go. *This is my fault.* Through the scrambling bodies and the beeping machines and her Uncle Dennis, in surgery scrubs, hugging her tightly as Annie's tears left a wet spot on the pale green fabric.

This is my fault.

I made us go.

I did this.

I ruined everything.

The fall had left Annie bruised and sore, but Paulo, who dropped from forty-one feet in the air, had smashed bones, severed tendons, and damaged several vital organs. His legs, pelvis, jaw, and right shoulder were all fractured from the blunt force, but his lungs had suffered the most damage; they were lacerated and bleeding from the crushing of his chest wall. A breathing tube was inserted to keep him going, but the images showed that neither lung could be sustained. He would need a new one to live. The doctors whispered about national registries and transplant lists and who could be called on such short notice. Which was when Annie, her mouth agape throughout the conversation, abruptly spoke up.

"Take mine."

"What?"

"My lung. You have to take it."

"Annie, it's not an option—"

"Yes, it is. It can save him!"

A debate quickly followed, as her uncle and others tried to convince Annie this was wrong. But she was screaming and resolute, and as a nurse she was versed in the minimum requirements for transplants, like blood type (which Annie and Paulo shared) and relative body sizes (they were the same height). She kept looking at Paulo through the doors of an operating room, surrounded by nurses and machinery. Paulo, who had saved her. Paulo, who was dying because of her.

"Annie, there's a risk—"

"I don't care—"

"Things can go wrong."

"I don't care!"

"He's in bad shape. Even if we succeed, he may not . . ."

"What?"

"Live."

Annie swallowed. "If he doesn't, I don't want to."

"Don't say that—"

"I mean it! Please, Uncle Dennis!"

She had been crying so much, she didn't think there were any tears left. But she remembered how happy she and Paulo had been two hours ago. Two hours? How can life change this much in two hours?

She repeated what Paulo had said in the back of the limousine, the words he had used to reassure her.

"We just got *married*..."

Her whole frame shook, and Dennis exhaled as if punched in the stomach. He turned to the senior surgeon, whose mouth was covered in an eggshell mask. He said a name they both knew, the top transplant expert at the hospital.

"I'll make the call," the senior surgeon said.

The rest of the details flew past like blowing rain. The rolling monitors, the wheels of the gurney, the alcohol wipes, the needles, the tubes. Annie ignored all of it, as if these were things happening to a shell around her. In the middle of a big crisis, a small belief can be your salvation. This was Annie's: she believed she could save her husband. She could make up for her mistake. *One lung each. We share.* She focused on that, as intensely as a trapped miner focuses on a beam of light.

Lying on the operating table, Annie said a prayer. *Let him live, God. Please let him live.* She felt the anesthesia taking over, her body going limp, her eyes closing. Her last conscious memory was of two hands on her shoulders, nudging her gently down, and a man's voice saying, "See you in a little bit."

Then the world was spinning and darkening, as if Annie were being lowered into a cave. Out of the blackness, she saw something strange. She saw the old man from her wedding running towards her, his arms outstretched.

Then everything went white.

Annie Makes a Mistake

She is two years old. She sits in a high chair. A green sippy cup is in front of her, filled with apple juice.

"Jerry, watch," her mother says as she removes the top. "She can drink from a straw."

"Wowee," her father mumbles.

"Kids her age can't do that."

"I'm busy, Lorraine."

"You're reading a newspaper."

"That's right."

Annie bounces.

"She wants your attention."

"I've seen her drink."

"She can use a straw."

"I heard you the first time."

"Please, Jerry? It'll only take a—"

"That's it. I gotta go." *He slaps down his newspaper. Annie hears the big noise he makes pushing his chair from the table.*

"Well," her mother says, unwrapping the straw, "let's practice so we can show him next time, OK?"

She touches Annie's soft cheek, and Annie, happy with the attention, swings her hand and knocks over the juice. It spills everywhere. She starts to cry.

"What'd you do to her?" Jerry yells from the hallway.

"Nothing!"

"Don't sound like nothing."

Her mother grabs a paper towel and wipes up the juice.

"It's all right, sweetie," she whispers to Annie. "Just an accident."

She kisses Annie on the cheek. As the front door slams, she looks down. "Just an accident," she repeats. "All gone now."

The Journey

Normally, when we come out of sleep, we open our eyes and everything resets. The dream world vanishes; the real world takes its place.

But this was not sleep, and what happened next to Annie was unlike any of her previous awakenings. Her eyes never opened, yet she could see quite clearly.

And she was moving.

The ground beneath her feet seemed to carve loose and zoom at tremendous speed, but with no friction, like a glass-enclosed elevator catapulted into space. She sped through colors of every shade, lavender and lemon and avocado green.

She felt no wind, but she *heard* wind. It seemed to come towards her in a rising squall, then pull away as if sucked through a tunnel, like a massive inhale and exhale. Oddly, this did not concern her. In fact,

Annie felt no worry at all. She felt almost airy, and as pain-free as a child.

Then something shot through her, something so alien she would not have had the words for it. Every piece of her was ill-fitting, as if her arms and legs had lengthened, and her head was on a new neck, and images flashed through her mind that had never been there before: the inside of a home, faces in a classroom, glimpses of the Italian countryside.

Then, just as quickly, she was back in her own consciousness and the colors were shooting by again, turquoise and yellow and salmon and wine red. She tried to find her way back to an idea, something about Paulo—*Paulo is hurt? Paulo needs me?*—but it felt as if she were swimming upstream against her memories. A balloon. A fire. A crash. A hospital.

"It could be good luck."

Is Paulo alive?

"We just got married."

Did I save him?

"See you in a little bit . . ."

Where am I?

Annie Makes a Mistake

She is four years old. She sits at the dinner table. Her parents are fighting. She plays with her fork.

"I can't believe you," her mother says.

"It just happened," her father says.

"Can I have a Creamsicle?" Annie asks.

"Go play, Annie," her mother mumbles.

"Go play," her father echoes.

"But can I have a Creamsicle?"

"Annie!"

Her mother rubs her forehead.

"What are we supposed to do?"

"We don't have to do nothing."

"Like the last time? Or the other times?"

"Daddy—?"

"Jesus, Annie!" her father yells. "Shut up!"

Annie's face drops. Her mother pushes from the table and hurries down the hall.

"Oh, yeah, great, run away," her father says, following after her. "What do you want from me? Huh?"

"I want you to remember you're married!" she yells.

Annie, now alone, slides from her chair. She tiptoes to the freezer. She pulls on the handle. With a thwock, *the door opens.*

The air is cold. But there it is: the box of Creamsicles. She wants one. She knows she's not supposed to. She sees two frozen Hershey's bars on the lower shelf. Her parents like those. She grabs one to bring to them. Maybe they will stop fighting. Maybe they will let her have a Creamsicle.

She steps back to watch the freezer door close— and is jerked up violently by two large hands.

"You stupid brat!" her father yells, as the Hershey's bar drops. "I told you not to do that!"

Annie feels a slap across her face and her eyes shut and the world goes black. Another slap. Tears ooze. Another. She cries so loudly her ears hurt.

"Stop it, Jerry!" her mother hollers.

"When I say no, I mean no!"

"Stop it!"

Another slap. Annie is getting dizzy.

"JERRY!—"

He lets go and Annie crumbles. Her parents scream as she sobs on the floor. She hears footsteps rushing her way. Then her mother is hovering over her, blocking the light.

The next morning, her father moves out. He slams the door as he goes. Annie knows why he's leaving. Because she wanted that Creamsicle. That's why he's going away.

The Arrival

Blue. Everything was blue. A single shade, enveloping Annie as if she'd been painted into it. She felt extremely light and strangely curious.

Where am I?

What happened?

Where is Paulo?

She could not see any part of herself. The blue was like a blanket covering all but her eyes. Suddenly, a large seat appeared in front of her, floating about chest-high, with a tan leather cushion and a silver rail across the top. It looked like something from a plane or a bus.

Annie instinctively went to touch it—and was shocked to see her right hand floating in front of her, unattached to anything else. No wrist. No forearm. No elbow. No shoulder. She realized the blue wasn't covering her body. She *had* no body. No middle or bottom. No stomach, thighs, or feet.

What is this?

Where is the rest of me?

What am I doing here?

Then, the blue around her wiped away, like soapy water rinsed from a glass, and there were snow-capped mountains to her left and urban skyscrapers to her right. Everything was zooming by, as if she were speeding while standing still. She looked down and saw tracks passing beneath her. She heard the wail of an unmistakable sound.

A train whistle.

She let go of the seat. It vanished. A second seat appeared, farther ahead. She gripped that one and it vanished, too, a new one materializing, guiding her forward. Finally, she reached a compartment door with an ornate bronze handle. She pulled it down.

With that, she went from outside to inside. An engine car sketched around her, as if being drawn by an artist's pen. The ceiling was low, the floor was riveted metal, and there were panels and gauges and levers everywhere. It looked like a train from the 1950s.

What kind of dream is this?

Why do I feel so light?

Where is everybody?

Something caught her eye. Up there. In the conductor's seat. A small head bounced into view, then was gone.

"Yes!" a young voice yelled. "Yes!"

Had this been a normal dream, Annie might have run, scared of a stranger the way we are often scared while sleeping. But danger has no grip in the afterlife, and Annie continued drifting forward until she was alongside the driver's seat. She looked down and saw something quite unexpected.

There, behind the steering console, was a young boy with caramel skin and jet-black hair, wearing a striped, short-sleeve shirt and a toy gun holster.

"Am I going too fast?" he asked.

Annie Makes a Mistake

She is six years old, walking home from school. She is accompanied, as usual, by three older kids: Warren Helms, who is eleven; his sister, Devon, who is nine; and his other sister, Lisa, who just turned eight.

"It's called Holy Communion," Lisa says.

"What do you do?" Annie asks.

"You go to church, you say you're sorry, and you eat a cookie."

"A wafer," Warren says.

"Then you get presents."

"Lots of presents," Devon says.

"Really?" Annie says.

"I got a bike," Warren says.

Annie feels jealous. She likes presents. She only gets them on Christmas and her birthday now. Her mother says they have to "tighten up" since her father left.

"Can I do a communum?"

"A Communion, stupid."

"You have to be Catholic. Are you Catholic?"

Annie shrugs. "I don't know."

"You'd know if you were Catholic," Warren says.

"How?"

"You just would."

Annie taps the sidewalk with her shoe. She feels the limits of being too young, a feeling she has often with the Helms kids, who walk her home every day. Most of her classmates are picked up by their mothers. But Annie's mother has to work, so Annie waits at the neighbors' until she gets home.

"Witch's house coming up," Warren says.

They look ahead to a small, brown, single-level home, with sagging gutters and a neglected front porch. Its paint is peeling. Its wood is rotted. The rumor is an old witch lives there and once, years ago, a kid went inside and never came out.

"Give you five dollars if you knock on her door," Warren says.

"Not me," Devon says.

"I don't need it," Lisa says. "I'm getting presents Sunday."

"Up to you, Annie."

Warren pulls a five-dollar bill from his pocket.

"You can buy a lot of stuff."

Annie stops. She thinks about presents. She stares at the door.

"She's probably not even home," Warren says. He waves the bill. "Fiiiive bucks."

"How many toys can I get for that?" Annie asks.

"A lot," Devon says.

Annie pulls on her curly hair and looks down, as if deciding. Then she lets go and marches up the path until she reaches the porch. She looks back at the others. Warren makes a knocking motion.

Annie inhales. Her heart is racing. She thinks again about presents. She lifts her fist to the screen door.

Before she can make contact, it swings open and a white-haired woman in a bathrobe is staring down at her.

"What do you want?" the woman croaks.

Annie can't move. She shakes her head as if to say, Nothing, she wants nothing. The woman looks past her to the other kids running away.

"They put you up to this?"

Annie nods.

"Can't you talk, girl?"

Annie swallows. "I wanted presents."

The old woman scowls.

"You shouldn't bother people."

Annie can't break her gaze from the woman's face, her long, slanted nose, her thin, cracked lips, the purplish circles under her eyes.

"*Are you really a witch?*" *Annie asks.*

The woman squints. "*No,*" *she says.* "*Are you?*"

Annie shakes her head.

"*I'm just sick, that's all,*" *the woman says.* "*Now go away.*"

She shuts the door. Annie exhales. She turns and runs to the others down the block. When she reaches them, she repeats what the woman said.

"*Deal's off,*" *Warren says.* "*She isn't a real witch.*"

Annie's shoulders slump.

She never gets the money.

The First Person Annie
Meets in Heaven

"Am I going too fast?"

Annie stared at the boy in the striped shirt.

Where am I?

"Can't hear you."

Where am I—

"Can't heaaaaarr you!"

I said—

He broke into a grin. "I can't hear you, stupid, because you're not talking."

He was right. Annie had no mouth. The words she was hearing were in her mind.

"Nobody can talk when they first arrive," the boy said. "It makes you listen better. That's what they told me, anyhow."

Who?

"The first people I met."

So you can *hear me?*

"What you're thinking, yeah."

Who are you?

"Sameer."

Why are you here?

"I kinda have to be."

Where am I?

"You still don't know?"

He pointed to the window and the shifting colors of the sky.

"Heaven."

I died?

"Boy, are you slow."

∽

Annie's thoughts were spilling everywhere, like raindrops down a windowpane. She died? Heaven? The balloon crash? Paulo?

Where is my body? Why am I like this?

"I don't know," the boy said. "Was someone on earth taking you apart?"

Annie thought about the transplant.

Sort of.

"That could do it. Hey. Watch this."

He pounded a flat button. The train whistle roared.

"I love that," he said.

Please. I don't belong here. I shouldn't have . . .

"What?"

You know.

"Died?"

Yes.

"Why not? I did."

But it wasn't my time. I'm not old or sick. I'm just . . .

"What?"

Annie replayed her wedding night, stopping for the motorist, which led to the balloon crash, which led to the transplant, which led to this.

A person who makes mistakes.

"Wow," the boy said, rolling his eyes. "Someone has self-esteem issues."

With that, he pushed the wheel and the train accelerated wildly, lifting into the air, dipping, rising, turning as sharply as a race car.

"Whoo-eee!" he yelled.

Annie spotted a purple ocean up ahead. As the

shoreline approached, she saw huge breaking waves and vast white foam.

Wait—

"Don't worry. I've done this a buncha times."

He dipped the train sharply and Annie braced for impact, but none came; just silent immersion and a boysenberry shade outside the windows.

"See?"

Where are we going?

"It's more like 'when.'"

He pulled the wheel upwards, and they emerged from the deep into what seemed to be a new world, more earthly in its appearance. The train slowed and joined a track by the edge of a small town, with tidy older houses of white aluminum siding.

"Get ready," the boy said. He punched out the front glass, which flew away in a thousand shattered pieces. He yanked the brake levers and the train screeched to a halt, as he and Annie launched through the opening.

"Whoo-hooo!" he yelled as they soared. "Cool, right?"

Then, somehow, they were standing by the tracks, no landing, no impact.

"Well, I thought it was cool," he mumbled.

❧

It was quiet now. The train was gone. Trees were barren and leaves covered the ground. The landscape turned a sepia patina, like an old film.

Please, Annie thought, *I don't understand.*

"What?"

Anything. Why I'm here. Why you're here.

"I'm here," the boy said, "because when you first get to heaven, you meet five people from your time on earth. They were all in your life for a reason."

What kind of reason?

"That's what you find out. They teach you something you didn't realize while you were alive. It helps you understand the things you went through."

So wait. You're my first person?

"Don't sound so excited."

I'm sorry. It's just—I don't know you.

"Don't be so sure."

The boy reached up and made a sweeping motion by Annie's eyes, and instantly, her face was back. Annie touched her cheeks.

What did you—

"Relax. I don't have cooties. Now watch. This is important."

He pointed to the tracks. Annie's vision was extremely sharp. Off in the distance, she saw a second train approaching, smoke coming from its stack. Beside it, a small boy was running to keep up, reaching out, stumbling, running again. Annie noticed his familiar features: black hair, caramel skin, striped shirt, cowboy holster.

Wait. That's you?

"Younger and dumber," the boy said.

What are you doing?

"I thought I could fly. I thought, 'I'll grab this train and hang on like a kite.'" He shrugged. "I was only seven."

The running boy made another failed lunge. The final car was about to pass. With a clenched jaw, he pumped his arms and gave a last leaping attempt. This time he hooked his fingers around a rail on the rear platform.

But only for an instant.

The speed of the train ripped his arm clean off his body, leaving the boy in the dirt, stunned and screaming, his shirtsleeve thickening with blood. The severed arm fell off the rail. It dropped to the gravel and reddened the stones.

The boy looked at Annie.

"Ouch," he said.

SUNDAY, 10:30 A.M.

The man named Tolbert signed a receipt. The woman behind the counter slid a copy back his way.

"All set," she said.

Tolbert waited for his wife's car to be brought around. Earlier, at the house, he had nudged her awake.

"I'll be back in a bit," he whispered.

"Hmm?—"

"Your tire was flat."

". . . it was?"

"I gotta buy a new one."

". . . OK . . ." She rolled over. "Be careful."

Now, as he glanced at the walls of the auto shop, Tolbert thought about the newlyweds who had stopped to help him last night. The groom, who changed the tire in his tuxedo, said the whole thing was his wife's idea. Nice guy. Funny guy. The incident had made Tolbert feel good about people. He didn't always feel that way.

A mechanic pulled up in the car.

"Good as new. Spare's in the trunk."

"Thanks," Tolbert said.

Once inside, Tolbert grabbed his cell phone and pressed the preset number for Teddy, his assistant.

It went to voice mail.

He dialed it again.

Same thing.

He dialed the office.

Voice mail again.

"Uch," he mumbled. "That damn kid."

He glanced in the rearview mirror, then turned the car around, heading for the balloon field instead of home, the good feeling about other people now gone.

The First Lesson

Annie stared at the wounded boy, lying in the gravel, missing an arm and bleeding profusely.

Why are you showing me this? It's awful.

"Yeah," Sameer said, "I never cried like that before. I sounded like a wolf."

Did you die?

"I would have. But . . ."

He pointed, and Annie saw a head poke out the train window, an older woman wearing black cat's-eye glasses. She ducked back inside.

The train slowed.

People jumped off.

They ran to the boy.

The woman ran, too.

She grabbed his severed arm, removed her jacket, and wrapped it tightly.

"Let's go to the next part," the boy said. "This is gross."

⟡

Instantly, they were in a hospital waiting room, where men smoked and women sewed and magazines on low tables were picked up without comment.

"This is 1961," the boy said. "That's my mom." He pointed to a woman in a red coat, her hands clasped against her lips. "And my pop," he added, noting a heavily whiskered man in a brown suit, hair the same black shade as his son's, his left leg shaking nervously. Annie saw the woman from the train. She was standing in the corner, arms crossed over her jacketless blouse.

When a doctor emerged, everyone turned. He exhaled and said something. Then he smiled widely, and the mother and father hugged and rose to grab the doctor's hands in gratitude.

Everything seemed to quicken then, like a movie being fast-forwarded. There were men with cameras and flashbulbs exploding and the mother and father beside the little boy in a bed.

"I made history," he told Annie.

History?

"First successful full reattachment of a limb." He grinned. "Pretty good for being stupid, huh?"

Annie watched the scenes unfold, the boy putting on his jacket, posing with a football, leaving the hospital, all of it captured by photographers and reporters.

Why am I seeing this?

"Because you went through the same thing."

How do you know?

"Know what?"

What happened to me?

"That's easy." He took her single hand. "I was there."

With that, he pulled Annie down a hospital corridor. The ceiling rose and the windows stretched like cellophane.

"The technique my doctors used became a new standard," the boy said. "Thanks to my ignorant chasing of a train, many future patients were healed."

Annie noticed his improved vocabulary. She looked at the narrow bridge of his nose and the thick bangs that fell loose and unkempt.

Why do you sound so . . . ?

"What?"

Grown-up?

The boy smiled.

"You got me."

Suddenly, the corridor rumbled and the two of them flipped and bounced as if shaken through a tube. The boy in the striped shirt was changing. When they dropped back down, he had morphed into a middle-aged man, his dark hair slicked back, his shoulders broad, his midsection large enough to push out a white medical coat.

What just happened?

"Remember that Bible verse? When I was a child, I spoke as a child, but now that I'm a man, la-da-da . . ."

You're a doctor?

"Well, I was. Heart attack. High blood pressure. Never think doctors take care of themselves better than patients."

He tugged on his coat and pointed to a name tag. "As I said, 'Sameer.' Or, if you prefer, Dr. Sameer. Titles seem kind of silly up here.

"By the way, sorry I called you stupid earlier. I picked my kid self to greet you. And I was a fairly obnoxious kid."

Annie felt dazed. She could barely keep up. She realized this was a different hospital now; the corridors were brighter. There was newer artwork on the walls.

Where are we?

"You don't remember?"

How could I remember? Isn't this your memory?

"Memories intersect."

They glided down a hallway and entered a private room. Sameer approached the patient in bed, a little girl with butterscotch curls whose left arm was bandaged from her elbow to her fingers.

"How are we doing, Annie?" he asked.

As the girl's mouth moved, Annie felt herself answer, "I'm scared."

Annie Makes a Mistake

She is eight years old and on the train to Ruby Pier. She wears cutoff shorts and a lime green T-shirt with a cartoon duck on the front. Her mother sits next to her, beside her latest boyfriend, Bob.

Bob has a thick mustache that covers his upper lip. Tony, the boyfriend before Bob, always wore sunglasses. Dwayne, the one before Tony, had a tattoo on his wrist. None of the boyfriends really speak to Annie. Only if she asks them something.

On the train, Bob takes her mother's hand and plays with it, but she pushes him off, nodding towards her daughter. Annie wonders if this means her mother doesn't like Bob.

They walk through the entrance of Ruby Pier, beneath spires and minarets and a giant arch. Annie gazes at the image of a woman in a high-collared dress holding a parasol—Ruby herself—welcoming guests to her park. After her father left, Annie and her mother came here often, just the two of them. They rode carousel horses and drank slushies and ate corn dogs. It was fun. But lately, boyfriends have been coming, too. Annie wishes it could go back to the way it was.

Her mother buys twenty tickets and warns Annie to stay away from grown-up rides like the roller coasters or Freddy's Free Fall. Annie nods. She knows the routine. She knows the snack bar. She knows the bumper cars. She knows her mother will go away with Bob and only come back at four o'clock, asking, "Did you have fun, Annie?" But she won't really care if Annie had fun.

By midafternoon the sun is hot, and Annie sits under a table umbrella. She is bored. The old man who fixes the rides walks past, the one with the patch on his uniform that says EDDIE and MAINTENANCE. He sits down across the way, looking around as if studying the rides.

Annie approaches, hoping he has pipe cleaners in his pocket.

"'Scuuuse me, Eddie Maint'nance?"

He sighs. "Just Eddie."

"Eddie?"

"Um-hmm?"

"Can you make me . . . ?"

She puts her hands together as if praying.

"C'mon, kiddo. I don't have all day."

When she asks for an animal, he begins twisting yellow pipe cleaners together. He hands her a figure, shaped like a rabbit, which she takes happily and runs back to the umbrella table.

She plays with it for a while. But soon she is bored again. It is only two o'clock. She walks to the midway and tries a game, throwing wooden rings at glass bottles. It costs her a ticket, but they give you a prize no matter what.

After three missed tosses, she is handed a small plastic package: inside is a balsa wood airplane. She fits one piece into the other. She throws it high. It flies in a loop. She does it again.

On her last toss, the plane glides over the heads of customers and lands on the other side of a railing, the one that blocks access to the base of Freddy's Free Fall. Annie looks both ways. The adults tower over her.

She slides under the rail.

She picks up the plane.

Then a woman screams.

Everyone is pointing at the sky.

SUDDENLY, it all made sense, who Sameer was, why they were in this hospital. Annie's spirit was inside her childhood body, lying in the hospital bed, looking out through youthful eyes. She wiggled her feet, covered in yellow hospital socks.

"You were my doctor," Annie whispered.

"Your voice is returning," Sameer said.

Annie coughed, trying to bring more heft to the words.

"I sound like a child."

"You work your way along in heaven."

"Why am I reliving this?"

"Because it all ties together. When I grew up, I realized how lucky I'd been. I got serious. I studied. I went to college, then medical school. I specialized in replantation."

Annie squinted. "Replantation?"

"A fancy word for reconnecting body parts."

"So you saved my hand?"

"Me and three other doctors. You only had a few hours. After that, it would have been too late."

Annie stared at her young, bandaged appendage.

"I can't remember the accident," she said. "I blacked the whole thing out."

"Understandable."

"And I'm really sorry, but I don't remember you."

Sameer shrugged. "Lots of kids don't remember their doctors. Starting with the ones who delivered them."

Annie studied the mature face before her, the jowls heavy with middle age, the temples flecked with gray hair. In the dark eyes, she saw the shadow of the impulsive boy.

"If this is really heaven," she asked, "why are you the person greeting me? Aren't I supposed to see God? Or Jesus? Or at least someone I remember?"

"That comes in time," Sameer said. "But the five people you meet first are chosen for a reason. They affected you in some way on earth. Maybe you knew them. Maybe you didn't."

"If I didn't know them, how could they affect me?"

"Ah." He patted his hands. "Now comes the teaching part."

He stepped around the bed and looked through the window.

"Tell me something, Annie. Did the world begin with your birth?"

"Of course not."

"Right. Not yours. Not mine. Yet we humans make so much of 'our' time on earth. We measure it, we compare it, we put it on our tombstones.

"We forget that 'our' time is linked to others' times. We come from one. We return to one. That's how a connected universe makes sense."

Annie looked at the white sheets and the blue blanket and the heavily bandaged hand that rested on her childhood belly. This was precisely when her life *stopped* making sense.

"Did you know," Sameer continued, "that hundreds of years ago, they used plaster and tape to reattach noses? Later they used wine and urine to preserve severed fingers. Reattaching rabbits' ears preceded efforts on humans. And not long before I was born, Chinese doctors trying replantation were still using needles that took two days to grind down.

"People lament that if their loved ones had been born fifty years later, they might have survived what killed them. But perhaps what killed them is what led someone to find a cure.

"Chasing that train was the worst thing I ever did—to myself. But my doctors used their knowledge to save me. And I advanced what they did on you. We tried a technique with your hand that we had never done before, allowing better blood flow through the arteries. It worked."

He leaned in and touched Annie's fingers, and she felt herself rising from inside her young body, returning to the mostly invisible form she had been before.

"Remember this, Annie. When we build, we build on the shoulders of those who came before us. And when we fall apart, those who came before us help put us back together."

He removed his white lab coat and unbuttoned his shirt, far enough to yank it down over his right arm. Annie saw the squiggly scars from decades ago, now faded to a milky white.

"Know me or not, we're part of each other, Annie."

He tugged the shirt back on.

"End of lesson."

Annie felt a tingling. Her left hand reappeared. For the first time in heaven, she felt pain.

"It won't hurt long," Sameer said. "Just a reminder."

"Of my loss?" she asked.

"Of your attachment," he replied.

❧

With that, they were back to where Annie had arrived in the afterlife, between the snowcapped mountains and the massive skyscrapers. A giant wheel of railroad track unfurled and Annie saw a train heading their way.

"This isn't how I pictured heaven," she said.

"Well," Sameer said, "you get to pick your eternal setting. On earth, trains haunted me. I never rode one again. But there's nothing to fear here. So I chose to flip my human existence. Now I ride this train wherever I please."

Annie looked at him blankly.

"Do you understand?" he said. "This isn't your heaven, it's mine."

The train arrived. Its doors slid open.

"Time to go."

"Where are we going?"

"Not 'we,' Annie. This stage of heaven, for me, is finished. But you have more to learn."

He rapped the exterior and put a foot on the step.

"Good luck."

"Wait!" Annie said. "My death. I was trying to save my husband. His name is Paulo. Did he live? Just tell me. Please. Tell me if I saved him."

The engine roared.

"I can't," Sameer said.

Annie looked down.

"But others are coming."

"*What* others?" Annie said.

Before he could answer, the train whisked off. The sky turned maroon. Then everything that surrounded Annie was sucked up into the air and spilled back down in a storm of grainy sand.

A vast brown desert surrounded her.

And she was alone.

Annie Makes a Mistake

Her hand is still bandaged from the accident three weeks ago, and her arm is in a sling to keep it elevated. She sits on her bed. There is little else to do. She is not allowed outside, and her mother, for some reason, has disconnected the TV set and cut its cord with scissors.

Annie walks to the window and sees Lorraine in the backyard, smoking. She has papers in her lap, but is staring at the laundry lines of neighboring houses. Sometimes, Annie notices, her mother has a hard time looking at her. Maybe parents want their children to be perfect. Annie studies her left hand, swollen and grotesque. She is not perfect anymore.

She hears something from downstairs. A knocking at the door. Strange. People usually ring the bell. Annie walks down the steps and hears the knocking again, soft, tentative. She turns the knob.

A woman is standing on the porch. She wears a bright red blazer, lip gloss, and thick pancake makeup that makes her skin a single shade.

"Oh, wow," the woman says. "You're Annie, right?"

Annie nods.

"How're you doing, sweetheart?"

"OK," Annie mumbles.

"We've been worried about you."

"Why?"

The woman, who keeps smiling, is motioning behind her back, as if pushing the air forward.

"Do you know how lucky you are?" she says.

"I don't feel lucky," Annie says.

"You don't? Well. That's understandable. Does your arm still hurt? Say, my friend is coming. Can you tell him—and me—about what happened?"

Annie is confused. She sees a man hurrying their way, carrying a large camera on his shoulders. She sees others behind him, running.

"Start with what you remember," the woman says. "You went to Ruby Pier and—"

Annie steps back. All these people are on the porch, pushing cameras and microphones at her face. Suddenly, she feels a jerk on her shirt. Her mother steps in front of her, pushing Annie back. Annie smells the cigarette smoke on her mother's clothes.

"Leave us alone!" her mother yells. "I'll call the police! I swear I will!"

She slams the door shut. She turns her angry face towards Annie.

"What have I told you! Do NOT answer the door! Never! Those people are vultures! Don't ever do that again! Do you understand me?"

Annie starts to cry. "I'm sorry . . . I'm sorry . . ."

Her mother tears up. Annie runs upstairs and slams her bedroom door. This is how it is now. Every day, one of them is crying. Annie hates it. She hates her hand. She hates her bandages. She hates the way people are acting towards her. She hates whatever happened at Ruby Pier, something she can't even remember.

The next morning, Annie's mother wakes her up early.

"Come on," she says, wearing a coat. "We're leaving."

The Next Eternity

Annie watched the sky turn to darker shades, gunmetal gray and mocha brown. Her left hand was stinging. The lightness she had experienced on her arrival was gone. She felt less like a child than a student, curious, tentative, as if she were growing up even after she died.

Alone in the desert, she saw a small pile in the distance, the only thing on an otherwise barren landscape. She used her two hands to pull herself through the sand.

When the pile drew close, Annie blinked to confirm what she was seeing: there, neatly stacked, were her feet, legs, arms, neck, and torso.

Her body in pieces.

What is going on? she thought. She tried to pull closer, but she suddenly could not. The sand wisped through her fingers like cotton candy. She looked around. A choking loneliness began to rise. Annie had felt this way often in the years after the accident, isolated, cast out, unable to do things. But why feel it here? Wasn't heaven supposed to be the end of such pain?

She remained still for what felt like a long time, until a distinct noise came from the flat quiet. It amplified rapidly, unrecognizable at first, then very recognizable.

It can't be, Annie thought. *A dog bark?* Yes. Then another. Then a cacophony of howls and yelps.

Annie turned to see the sand kicking up and small dust clouds to her left and right. Quickly, an army of canines—every breed and size—encircled her, barking excitedly, grabbing at her body pieces and tossing them into the air.

Annie put her hands to her ears. "Stop it!" she screamed. Her voice was deeper than it had been with Sameer, but it had no effect on the animals. They growled and yipped and whipped up sand everywhere.

A brown Labrador dangled one of Annie's feet in its jowls. "No!" Annie screamed, tugging it free. "That's mine!" An Afghan hound, with long stringy fur, raced past with her other foot. "Give it!" she yelled, wrestling it loose.

Suddenly, as if on cue, the dogs packed together and raced to the horizon, taking the rest of Annie's body with them.

"No, wait!" she heard herself yell.

The dogs looked back, as if urging her to follow. Annie scanned the otherwise barren desert. Whatever was out there had to provide more answers than this. She placed her two loose feet in front of her. She willed herself up until it felt as if she were standing.

"Come on," she said to herself.

And she began to run.

The Second Person Annie Meets in Heaven

Over the centuries, man has created countless depictions of the hereafter; few, if any, show the departed soul alone. Despite the ways we isolate ourselves on earth, in our final bliss, we are always with someone: the Lord, Jesus, saints, angels, loved ones. A solitary afterlife seems unimaginably grim.

Perhaps this is why Annie chased the dog pack through heaven, without knowing where it might take her. She followed the animals up a sharp incline, over a ridge, and down into a valley. The sky above her shifted again, from mustard to plum to forest green. These colors, and all the firmament's colors since her arrival, reflected the emotions of her life on earth, replaying as that life was replayed. But Annie could not know this.

Instead, she continued her pursuit until the dogs broke from their pack and spread like spokes of a wheel. The ground split into a checkerboard of small green lawns, each with a door of various design, wood, metal, painted, stained, some modern, some ancient, some rectangular, some rounded at the top. The dogs sat obediently, one outside each entrance, as if waiting for someone to come through.

"Annie," a breathy voice said. "At last."

Annie spun to see an elegant old woman. She looked to be in her eighties or nineties, with thick silver hair, a sloped nose, a tucked chin, and large, sad eyes. She wore a knee-length fur coat and a necklace dotted with colorful stones.

"Who are *you*?" Annie said.

The woman seemed disappointed.

"You don't remember?"

Annie studied her smiling face, the skin wrinkled and sagging.

"Are you . . ."

The woman cocked her head.

". . . my second person?"

"Yes."

Annie sighed. "I'm sorry. I don't know you, either."

"Well, you were having a tough time when we met."

"When was that? What were we doing? If you were in my life, why does none of this make sense to me?"

"Hmm."

The old woman paced, as if thinking of options. Then she stopped and pointed to the blue horizon, where a car was heading towards them.

"Let's go for a ride."

Instantly, Annie was in the passenger seat. She was alone. No one was driving. The car sped through cottony clouds and glaring sunshine. The old woman ran alongside the vehicle, peering through the window.

"Don't you want to get in?" Annie yelled.

"No, it's fine!" the woman yelled back.

Eventually (although Annie could not measure time in heaven—it felt like everything was happening quickly yet taking forever) the car stopped. Annie got out. The old woman stood beside her, breathing heavily. There was a one-story structure by a dirt parking lot. A blue-and-white sign read PETUMAH COUNTY ANIMAL RESCUE SHELTER.

"I remember this building," Annie whispered. "This is where we got my dog."

"That's right," the woman said.

"Cleo."

"Uh-huh."

"This was your place?"

"At the time."

The old woman sat down.

"What else do you remember?"

What Annie remembered was this: after living her whole life in the same house, on the same street, she and her mother abruptly left—just got in the car and sped away, their possessions in suitcases or big black garbage bags, the trunk held shut by a bungee cord.

They drove for days, eating at gas stations or fast-food places. They slept in the car. They finally stopped in a state called Arizona, where, for a while, they lived in a roadside motel, which had pale green carpeting and a lock on the telephone.

After that, they moved to a trailer. It sat on large blocks in a treeless park, alongside other trailers. They slept, ate, bathed, and washed their clothes inside. Their only contacts with the outside world were visits to a supermarket, the local library (to get

Annie books), and a nearby hospital, where Annie had her bandages replaced and her splints adjusted. Annie still could not use her left hand; sometimes she couldn't feel the tips of her fingers. She wondered if for the rest of her life she would have to do what she was doing now, carrying everything one-handed, using her elbow to hold things open.

Meanwhile, the rules of life had battened down. Annie was not allowed in the park alone. She was not allowed to walk in socks (lest she slip). A skateboard was deemed too dangerous, as was tree climbing and most playground equipment. Alone much of the time, Annie read her library books, wedging them into her weakened left hand and turning the pages with her right.

One morning, Lorraine took Annie to a courthouse, where they had to sign papers.

"Why?" Annie asked her mother.

"We're changing our name."

"I'm not Annie anymore?"

"Our last name."

"Why?"

"It doesn't matter."

"Why?"

"I'll explain later."

"When?"

❧

She never got an answer. Instead, months passed at the trailer park and Annie grew miserable. It was always hot in Arizona and the people in the park were old and boring. Lorraine did not talk to the neighbors. She told Annie not to, either. At night, Annie heard her mother crying in her bedroom. It made Annie angry.

I'm the one who got hurt, she thought.

This was the start of a silent resentment. It made Annie feel more alone, which only increased her bitterness. The more Lorraine cried, the less Annie could think of to say to her.

For a while, the two of them barely spoke. Emboldened by her anger, Annie began defying the rules, slipping out when Lorraine was gone. She had read in a library book that you could grow new flowers by planting a leaf off an old one. So Annie snuck scissors under her T-shirt and snipped leaves from a neighbor's garden. She put them in small holes and poured Dixie cups of water over the top of them. She did this for weeks, looking for any sign of life. If she heard a car approaching, she would duck back into the trailer.

But one afternoon, she moved too slowly. Her

mother, coming home from work, saw Annie pulling the trailer door shut.

The next day, it was locked from the outside.

Things went on this way. One night, while eating in the trailer's tiny kitchen, it was so quiet, Annie could hear Lorraine's chewing.

"Am I ever going to school?" Annie asked.

"Not for a little while."

"How come?"

"I have to figure out work."

"But I don't know anyone here."

"I know."

"When are we going home?"

"We're not."

"Why? I don't have any friends! I want to go *home*!"

Annie's mother swallowed and rose silently. She scraped her plate into the sink. Then she walked to the bedroom, just a few feet away, and shut the door.

The next morning, she woke Annie early and made scrambled eggs with shredded cheese. She pushed them onto Annie's plate without comment. When Annie finished, Lorraine announced, "We're going for a ride."

It was raining lightly, and Annie kept her arms crossed the entire trip, her mouth in a scowl. Eventually, the car pulled in to a dirt parking lot, with a one-story building and a blue-and-white sign that read PETUMAH COUNTY ANIMAL RESCUE SHELTER.

They walked towards the back. Annie heard barking. Her eyes widened.

"Are we getting a *dog*?" she asked.

Her mother stopped. Her face seemed to crumble. She bit her lip and blinked back tears.

"What's the matter, Mommy?" Annie asked.

"You're smiling," her mother said.

That day, Annie walked past dozens of rescued or abandoned dogs. She watched them leap and paw at the cage doors. The woman running the shelter said Annie could choose any dog she wanted, so Annie studied them carefully. She played with several, letting them lick her cheeks and fingers. At the end of a row, she saw a cage with three cocoa-and-white puppies. Two ran for the door, barking on their hind legs. The third remained in the back. It wore a plastic funnel around its neck.

"What's that?" Annie asked.

"An Elizabethan collar," the woman said. "To keep the dog from biting or licking."

"Biting or licking what?" Lorraine asked.

"Her wound. She needed surgery when we found her." The woman jangled her keys. "A tough story."

Lorraine touched Annie's shoulder. "Come on, sweetie, there's others to look at."

But Annie was fixated. She felt something for this creature, wounded as Annie was wounded. She tilted her head the way the dog's head was tilted. She made small kissing sounds. The dog stepped forward.

"Do you want to play with her?" the woman asked.

Annie's mother shot her an annoyed look, but the woman opened the cage door.

"Come here, Cleo," she said. "Someone wants to meet you."

❧

As Annie recounted this story to the old woman, the image appeared before them. The shelter owner had long, silver-tinged hair and wore blue jeans, black sneakers, and a faded flannel shirt. She smiled as she handed the collared dog to Annie.

"Is that you?" Annie asked.

"Yes," the old woman said.

Annie looked around.

"Where's my mother? She brought me here."

"This is your heaven, Annie, and where it intersects with mine. Others are not included."

That made Annie hesitate. She braced herself.

"Did I do something to you?"

"Well, yes."

"Am I here to make amends?"

"Amends?"

"For my mistake. Whatever it was."

"Why do you assume it was a mistake?"

Annie didn't say what she was thinking: that her whole life, she'd been making mistakes.

"Tell me about Cleo," the old woman said.

The truth was, for nearly a year, Cleo, part beagle, part Boston terrier, was Annie's primary companion. Lorraine could only find part-time work, morning shifts at an auto-parts factory; she was gone by the time Annie woke up and didn't return until the afternoon. Annie hated having to call her mother every morning and tell her that she'd eaten breakfast. She especially hated hanging up and being alone. With Cleo, there was finally another presence in the trailer—a furry, foot-tall presence, with floppy brown ears and a mouth that curled like a smile beneath her muzzle.

That first day after the shelter visit, Annie poured a bowl of cereal for herself and a bowl of pellets for her new dog. She watched Cleo try to eat with the awkward collar. The surgery wound near her shoulder was still red. How did that happen? Annie wondered. Did she run into something sharp? Did another dog attack her?

Cleo whined as the collar blocked her access. Annie was not supposed to take it off; her mother had told her six times. But the dog looked at Annie as if begging for help, and Annie felt so bad that she leaned over and, with her good hand, undid the clasp. Cleo surged to the bowl.

When all the pellets were eaten, Annie tapped her thighs, and Cleo scrambled her way. She crawled into Annie's lap and sniffed her splinted fingers. Even when redirected, the dog returned to Annie's injury, licking and poking it with her muzzle.

"You want to see?" Annie said. She took her arm out of the sling. Cleo licked the skin around her wrist and whimpered. Something stirred inside Annie, as if the dog understood more than a dog should.

"It still hurts," Annie whispered. "And I don't even know what I did."

She realized she was crying. Perhaps because she had said the words out loud. *I don't even know what I did.* The more Annie cried, the more the dog whined with her, lifting its snout to lick the tears away.

"Did you know," the old woman said now, standing beside the grown-up Annie, "that a dog will go to a crying human before a smiling one? Dogs get sad when people around them get sad. They're created that way. It's called empathy.

"Humans have it, too. But it gets blocked by other things—ego, self-pity, thinking your own pain must be tended to first. Dogs don't have those issues."

Annie watched her younger self rub her cheek against Cleo's snout.

"I was so lonely," Annie whispered.

"I could tell."

"I lost everything I knew."

"I'm sorry."

"Did you ever feel that way?"

The woman nodded. "Once."

"When?" Annie asked.

The woman pointed to the trailer window.

Annie stepped up. She did not see the outside. Instead, through the glass, she viewed a darkened

room in an abandoned house. There was no furni-
ture. A window was smashed. Graffiti was sprayed
on the rear wall. In the corner, Annie saw a pair of
eyes, barely catching the light. Annie realized it was
a large mother dog, lying on the dirty floor, surrounded by puppies nuzzling her belly.

"She gave birth a week earlier," the old woman
said.

"Why is she in this house?"

Before the old woman could answer, the door
burst open, and two men in T-shirts, jeans, and
boots, one wearing a ski hat, stumbled inside, holding cans of beer. They recoiled when they heard the
growl of the mother dog.

The man in the ski hat went wobbly for a moment.
Then he pulled a gun from the rear of his pants.

"No . . ." Annie whispered.

The man fired three times, each bullet creating a
small burst of orange light. The men laughed. They
swigged from their cans, then fired again. After five
more shots, they staggered out the door.

"What happened?" Annie said. "What just *happened*?"

The old woman looked away. Annie heard muffled laughter coming from outside, and whining,

high-pitched squeals from the corner. She saw the puppies pawing at their now lifeless mother. Tears rolled down Annie's face.

"They killed her?"

"And some of her babies," the old woman said. "Three survived."

"The poor mother."

"Yes. That was the last time I saw her."

Annie blinked. "*What* did you say?"

The woman pulled back the collar of her coat and leaned forward to reveal an old gunshot wound on her shoulder. She touched Annie's teary cheeks.

"I cried for you. You cry for me."

Annie Makes a Mistake

She pulls a T-shirt over her head and clips a leash on Cleo.

"Let's go, girl."

It is eight months since the accident. Annie's bandages are gone. So is Cleo's plastic collar. New fur has grown around Cleo's wound. But Annie's hand is rippled with red scars and discolored by uneven circulation. The fingers often curl involuntarily, making it look like a claw. Annie wishes she could grow fur on top of her scars like Cleo had.

"Now stay with me," Annie says, mounting her bicycle. "Don't go running ahead."

She is not supposed to ride without her mother. She is not supposed to take Cleo beyond the trailer park. But being alone has made her resourceful. And there is something she wants to see.

"Come on, girl. Here we go . . ."

As she pedals, the dog romps alongside, and she steers mostly one-handed, a skill she has developed. They cut through a small wooded area, down a street, and beyond some hedges. Annie stops and sets her bike on its kickstand. She walks down a hill, Cleo beside her. They reach a fence and Annie hooks her fingers into the links.

In front of her is a school. Recess is about to start. Annie knows this. She has been here before.

A bell rings and children spill out the doors. They scatter around swing sets. Some kick a ball. Their voices are loud and happy-sounding. Annie crouches lower. She spots two girls who look her age wandering off to the side of the building. One has straight blond hair and is wearing black jeans and pink sneakers. Annie wishes she had pink sneakers.

"Stay here," Annie whispers. She wraps Cleo's leash around the fence. Cleo whines, but Annie says, "Shhh!" and tiptoes off.

She passes along the perimeter of the fence. She goes around a bend where the ground is new mulch, wet from a sprinkler. She sees the two girls now, leaning against the school wall. One takes something from her pocket and applies it to the other's mouth. Lipstick? Curious, Annie climbs atop a tree stump for a better view. The girls are gazing into something and making faces—a mirror, maybe?—and Annie wonders what color lipstick it is.

Suddenly, the girls turn her way and Annie loses

her balance. She falls and lands on her bad hand, a jolt of pain shooting through her. She bites her lower lip. Wet mulch sticks to her arms. She doesn't move, fearful the girls might approach.

Finally, the bell rings and the voices disappear. Annie rises slowly, her wrist throbbing, and trudges back to where she left Cleo.

When she gets there, the dog is gone.

Her heart begins to race. "Cleo?" she yells. "Cleo?"

She runs the length of the fence. Nothing. She runs back. Nothing. She runs up the hill to her bicycle. Nothing. She spends the next hour circling the same streets, tears burning her eyes, yelling Cleo's name and praying she'll hear barking in return.

Finally, knowing her mother will be back soon, she pedals home, sobbing. When she reaches the trailer, she stops. She exhales. There, sitting against the door, is Cleo, her leash trailing like a leather snake.

"Oh, Cleo, come here!" Annie says as the dog races to her, leaping into her grasp and licking the mulch on her arms. This is better, Annie thinks, a dog who loves me, a dog who's happy to see me, better than those girls and their stupid lipstick, better any day of the week.

The Second Lesson

Annie stared at the old woman in the coat.

"Are you saying . . . ?"

"I'm Cleo."

"But you're a *woman*."

"I thought this form would be easier."

"The shelter owner. I asked if that was you—"

"She was holding me. You asked if 'that' was me. Or I thought that's what you asked. Sorry. We often think things are about us when they are not."

Annie studied the woman's sagging skin, the sloped nose, the gaps between her teeth.

"Cleo," she whispered.

"Yes."

"We're communicating."

"We always communicated. Didn't you know when I was hungry? When I was scared? When I wanted out?"

"I guess," Annie said. "And you? You understood when I spoke to you?"

"Not your words. But your intent. Dogs hear differently than humans; we detect emotion in your voices. Anger, fear, lightness, heaviness—I could tell those from your sound. I could smell your day on your skin. What you ate. When you'd showered. The times when you sprayed your mother's perfume on your wrists. Remember? You would sneak into her room and sit by her mirror and hold your hand out for me to sniff?"

Annie stared hard into Cleo's eyes, trying to imagine the rest of her, her cocoa fur, her thin, floppy ears. She recalled the things Cleo recalled. She recalled Cleo getting older. She even recalled the day Cleo died, driving to the vet's office in her mother's car, a sluggish Cleo breathing slowly in her lap. But she did not know how these memories could matter now.

"Why are you here, Cleo?" Annie asked.

"To teach you something. Each soul you meet in heaven does the same."

"So animals have souls?"

Cleo looked surprised.

"Why wouldn't they?" she said.

⁂

The landscape suddenly shifted. They were out of the trailer, away from the abandoned house. They were floating now in a pale green sky, atop what appeared to be a massive mattress, with orange sheets and pink pillows that looked like small hills.

"Wait," Annie said. "This is my old bed . . ."

"That's right."

"It's huge."

"Well, that's how it looked to me. I had to run and leap when you called me."

"Why are you—"

"Loneliness, Annie. That's what I am here to explain. You suffered it. You tortured yourself over it. But you never understood it."

"What's to understand about being lonely?" Annie snapped. "It's terrible."

"Not always. Do you think, if you hadn't felt so lonely, you would have chosen me at the shelter? Or taken off my collar to let me eat that first morning? Your loneliness gave me a home. And happiness.

"Remember what I said about empathy? It works both ways. I was wounded. Different. And you felt . . ."

Annie glanced at her detached left hand.

"Wounded," she whispered. "Different."

"And . . . ?"

"Alone."

The woman nodded towards the giant pillows, and Annie saw a thousand nights of her childhood, cradling her beloved companion.

"Not alone," Cleo said.

The landscape changed once more, back to the checkerboard lawns Annie had seen earlier and the countless dogs waiting patiently by the doors.

"Have you ever considered how many living things there are on earth?" Cleo asked. "People. Animals. Birds. Fish. Trees. It makes you wonder how anyone could feel lonely. Yet humans do. It's a shame."

She looked to the sky, now a deep shade of purple. "We fear loneliness, Annie, but loneliness itself does not exist. It has no form. It is merely a shadow that falls over us. And just as shadows die when light changes, that sad feeling can depart once we see the truth."

"What's the truth?" Annie asked.

"That the end of loneliness is when someone needs you." The old woman smiled. "And the world is so full of need."

With that, all the doors on all the lawns swung open, revealing countless grim-faced people, children on crutches, adults in wheelchairs, soldiers in dirt-stained uniforms, widowed women in veils. Annie sensed they were all in need of comfort in some way. The dogs sprang to them, tails wagging. They licked and nuzzled the sad people and were embraced and cradled in return. The grim faces melted into grateful smiles.

"This is my heaven," Cleo said.

"Watching people come home?" Annie asked.

"Feeling the joy when they do. Souls reuniting. It's something divine."

"But it happens every day."

Cleo tilted her head. "Don't divine things happen every day?"

Annie watched the happy greetings with a twinge of regret. The afterlife, clearly, was to be filled with others; she could see that now. But her afterlife meant being without Paulo, the person she loved most. How could she ever be content?

"What is it, Annie?"

"My husband. I was trying to keep him alive. I don't know if I did. All I remember is the operating room, a doctor's hands on my shoulders, him saying, 'See you in a little bit.' But then, nothing."

Annie struggled with the words. "I'm all right with dying as long as Paulo lived. Just tell me my death wasn't wasted."

The old woman smiled.

"No act done for someone else is ever wasted."

With that, Cleo nodded to a final door, and as it swung open, Annie saw her nine-year-old self jump off her bicycle and run to hug Cleo the day she thought she lost her.

At the same time, the old woman leaned in to Annie, and a sudden warmth oozed through Annie's fingers and palms. Her wrists reappeared, then her elbows, biceps, and shoulders.

"My arms," Annie marveled. "They're back."

"To hold what you love," Cleo whispered.

Then, in Annie's new grasp, Cleo's womanly frame shrank down. Her coat tightened and became her fur. Her legs pulled in. Her ears and snout elongated. She was revealed as the puppy she used to be on earth, and she panted as Annie held her up and said, "There you are. Cleo. Cleee-o!"

Annie's mind was flooded with memories: Cleo running alongside Annie's bicycle, Cleo snapping pizza from Annie's plate, Cleo rolling over as Annie tickled her belly. She felt a joy she had not known in years. After all this time, after all the disappointments and letdowns, Annie was holding her old dog again. Maybe Cleo was right; maybe reunion was heaven-sent.

"Good girl," Annie whispered, feeling a grateful tongue lap against her cheeks. "Good girl." She closed her eyes to revel in the old sensation.

When she opened them, her hands were empty, and she was alone in the desert once more.

SUNDAY, 11:14 A.M.

Tolbert was furious. He'd been calling Teddy, his assistant, for nearly an hour. No response.

How do you not answer the phone? What if I was a customer? Tolbert swore he would fire Teddy when he saw him, even though it wasn't easy to find balloon pilots these days.

Tolbert himself had come to ballooning late, when he was fifty-two, after retiring from a naval career. He'd been a pilot early on, and even when they said he was too old to fly, he maintained his interest in aviation. A balloon wasn't exactly a fighter jet, but it got him in the skies and employed familiar areas of expertise: wind and weather analysis, equipment inspection. And Tolbert liked that you could work by yourself.

Well, almost, he thought now as he stewed over Teddy's irresponsibility, *almost by yourself.*

He turned his wife's car down a dirt road, a few miles from the barn that stored the balloon equipment. He squinted. Then he slammed on the brakes.

Up ahead were four police cars blocking the road, their lights flashing.

An officer was waving Tolbert in.

The Next Eternity

Heavy winds blew the desert sands away and Annie felt herself rising into swirling shades of scarlet and rose. She spun like a pocketwatch on a chain. Then, for the first time in heaven, Annie fought back. She flailed as if trying to detach from a hook. Her legs had returned, and she used them to kick, until a final surge broke her loose and she fell.

She fell through open air and through coral-colored clouds, until she saw below her a large pink island, with five peninsulas jutting out like spokes. She braced for a hard impact, but at the last instant, she flipped over and landed softly on her back.

She was lying in pink snow.

"Hello?" Annie yelled, her voice echoing in a teenaged timbre. "Is anyone here?"

She flapped her arms and legs to ensure everything was functioning. She rose to her feet. Annie felt older now, stronger; it seemed she was reconstructing her earthly body as she advanced through heaven. Her thoughts were maturing as well. An edginess had come over her, a young adult's impatience. She wanted answers.

She looked down at the frozen pink surface.

Her imprint had created a snow angel.

Annie glanced around. Was anyone coming to greet her? She began to walk, then she jogged, then she ran, lifting her knees to shake the snow loose. She flashed on her childhood winters, and suddenly she was wearing her old fuchsia jacket, fur boots, and black ski pants, as if the memory had dressed her.

The snow went on as far as she could see. The sky was streaks of cinnamon light. Annie ran towards the peninsulas until she felt exhausted. She shut her eyes to gather her thoughts.

When she opened them, she saw the snow angel back in front of her. Only this time, where the head was indented, there were two eyes looking out.

Annie moved slightly. The eyes followed.

"Are you here for me?" Annie asked, tentatively.

"Are you here for me?" a voice echoed.

Annie looked around.

"Do I know you?" Annie said.

"Do I know you?" it echoed again.

Annie leaned in and squinted. The eyes squinted back. Annie recoiled. She saw these eyes every day in the mirror.

"You're . . . me?" Annie said.

No response.

"Say something."

The eyes stared upwards.

"What are you looking at?"

With that, the pink snow rumbled and the five peninsulas curled in like fingers. Annie realized she was not on an island at all, but inside the palm of a giant hand.

"Hello, sweetheart."

Annie trembled. *No*, she thought, recognizing the voice immediately. She raised her eyes to where the angel's eyes were looking, and the sky filled with the most familiar face of her life.

"Mom?" Annie whispered. "Is it you?"

Annie Makes a Mistake

She is twelve years old. She is starting middle school. She hopes it will be better than elementary school. By the time Lorraine finally enrolled Annie, it was midway through third grade. Annie was "the new kid." On her first day, the teacher distributed art supplies, and, unable to grip tightly with her left hand, Annie dropped them in front of everyone. The other kids laughed.

"Now, class," the teacher warned, "just because a student is different, that's no reason to act differently towards them," which Annie knew was an invitation to do exactly that. Her self-consciousness grew.

As the weeks passed, she tried to make friends, sometimes through gifts. She snuck bags of chocolate chip cookies from home and handed them out during recess. One day she heard some girls talking about Smurf dolls, and on a trip to the store with her mother, she shoplifted a box of them, hiding them under her sweatshirt. She gave those out, too—until a teacher noticed and called Annie's mother, who was mortified and dragged Annie back to the store and made her apologize to the manager.

All through fourth grade, and much of fifth and sixth, Annie had to wear splints to keep her fingers straight. The ugly purple scars drew looks, and Annie developed a habit of hiding her left hand whenever possible—behind her back, in a jacket pocket, shielded by a notebook. She often wore long sleeves despite the Arizona heat.

Her mother insisted she do her rehabilitation exercises multiple times a day, making the thumb touch each finger, as if forming the OK sign. She did these at her desk, hoping no one would notice, until the time she got in an argument with a girl named Tracy.

"OK, Annie, OK!" Tracy yelled, mimicking the signs with her hands. Others laughed. It became Annie's nickname, "OK Annie." Most of the kids called her that now.

Paulo—the boy she met during leapfrog—never did. Annie felt safe around him. He smiled a lot and seemed confident. One day, in the cafeteria, he leaned over and lifted her hand into his, without even asking.

"It's not that bad," he said.

"It's gross," she replied.

"I've seen worse."

"Where?"

"I saw a picture of a guy who got attacked by a bear. That was gross."

Annie almost laughed.

"I didn't get attacked by a bear."

"You couldn't. There's no bears in Arizona."

This time Annie did laugh.

"Would you change it back?" Paulo asked.

"You mean back to normal?"

"Yeah. If you could?"

"Are you kidding? Totally."

"I don't know." He shrugged. "It makes you different."

That's the problem, Annie thought. Still, she appreciated Paulo's compassion. As she got to know him, she learned he liked football and outer-space stuff. On a trip to the library, Annie rifled through the astronomy books until she found one with a chapter on the northern lights, something he talked about a lot. The next day, before class began, she put the book down on Paulo's desk.

"Look what I found," she said.

His mouth curled into a smile. "What?"

"Just something I'm reading."

She flipped open to the chapter, and Paulo's eyes

*widened and he said, "No way!" Annie felt warm
inside, and she pushed the book towards him.*

"For you."

"I thought you were reading it."

"I can read it when you're done."

*"Cool," he said, taking it. Then he added, "Thanks
a lot, Annie."*

Not OK Annie. Just Annie

*With the two of them now in middle school, Annie
hopes she can see Paulo more, but her mother contin-
ues to control her every move; she drops Annie off
each morning, and every afternoon she is parked in
front of the main entrance, beeping her horn. Annie
lowers her head and walks rigidly to the car, certain
she hears other kids laughing.*

*One day, with classes finished, Annie is standing
in the front vestibule, looking through the glass. A
group of pretty girls is just outside, all with purple
backpacks slung over their shoulders. Annie hesitates. She doesn't want her mother to honk while
these girls are around.*

"Waiting them out?" Paulo says.

Annie looks up, flushed. "Is it that obvious?"

"Come on. I want to talk to your mom."

Before Annie can react, Paulo is already out the door. He strides confidently as Annie hurries to keep up. She sees the backpack girls staring.

When he reaches the car, Paulo leans towards the window and offers his hand. "Hi, Annie's mom, I'm Paulo."

Lorraine hesitates. "Hello, Paulo."

"Now that we're in this new school, I can walk home with Annie so you don't have to drive her every day. I don't live too far from you."

Annie's heart races. Paulo wants to walk home together?

"Thank you, Paulo," Lorraine says. "But we're fine. Come on, Annie, we've got errands to run."

Annie doesn't want to go. She doesn't want to open the door. Paulo does it for her. She slowly ducks inside and reluctantly lets him close it.

"If you change your mind . . ." Paulo says.

They drive off.

"Bye!" he yells.

Annie feels her skin get hot. She had wanted nothing more than what Paulo just proposed, and her mother shot it down without a thought.

"Why did you have to be so mean to him?" Annie snaps.

"*What are you talking about? I wasn't mean.*"

"*Yes, you were!*"

"*Annie—*"

"*You were!*"

"*He's just a boy—*"

"*God, Mom! Why do you have to be here all the time? I'm so sick of you! You treat me like an infant! You're the reason I have no friends!*"

Her mother squeezes her lips, as if biting back something she wants to yell. She shifts her hands on the steering wheel.

"*Do your exercises,*" *she says.*

The Third Person Annie
Meets in Heaven

"Mom?" Annie whispered.

Her mother's face laid claim to the sky. It was everywhere Annie looked. Annie realized how natural it felt saying that word, *Mom*, yet how long it had been since she'd felt it pass her lips.

"Hello, angel," her mother replied, a phrase she had used when Annie was small. Her voice seemed to be pressed to Annie's ears.

"Is it really you?"

"Yes, Annie."

"We're in heaven?"

"Yes, Annie."

"Did you go through this, too? Meeting five—"

"Annie?"

"Yes?"

"Where is the rest of you?"

Annie looked at her hollow middle, visible now through the winter jacket. Her voice quivered.

"I made a mistake, Mom. There was an accident. A crash. Paulo. I was trying to save Paulo. Remember Paulo? From school? We got married. We had one night together. Then a balloon ride. It was my fault—"

Annie stopped and dropped her head, as if the weight of the story were draped on top of it.

"Look up, sweetheart," Lorraine said.

Annie did. Her mother's skin was flawless. Her lips were full, her thick auburn hair dark at the roots. Annie had nearly forgotten how beautiful her mother once was.

"Why are you so big?" Annie whispered.

"That's how you saw me on earth. But it's time you see me as I saw myself."

Her giant hand lifted, then tilted down towards her face. Annie stumbled forward, into her mother's eyes, which opened like a deep well, swallowing her whole.

⁓

Children begin by needing their parents. Over time, they reject them. Eventually, they become them.

Annie would go through all those stages with Lorraine. But, like many children, she never knew the backstory of her mother's sacrifice.

Lorraine was only nineteen when she met Jerry, who was twenty-six. She worked in a bakery; he drove a bread truck. Lorraine had never traveled more than thirty miles from her small town, and she dreamed of escaping its boredom and the stiff, high-cut uniform she wore every day. One evening, Jerry showed up in a suede jacket and engineer boots and suggested they go for a ride. They drove through the night, and didn't stop until they reached the East Coast. They drank. They laughed. They splashed barefoot in ocean waves. They used Jerry's jacket as a blanket on the sand.

Three weeks later, they were wed, in a civil ceremony in a downtown courthouse. Lorraine wore a paisley dress. Jerry wore a maroon sports jacket. They toasted each other with champagne and spent the weekend in a beachside motel, going for swims and drinking wine in bed. Their passion was strong, but like most passions, it burned fast. It was already waning when, a year later, Annie was born.

Jerry was not present for the birth. He was out of town on an overnight truck run that somehow turned into five days of absence. Lorraine's brother, Dennis, drove her home from the hospital.

"I can't believe he's not here," Dennis grumbled.

"He'll come," Lorraine said.

But as the days passed, he did not. Lorraine was getting calls, friends wanting to visit, asking the baby's name. Lorraine knew the name she wanted. It was inspired by a woman her grandmother used to talk about, Annie Edson Taylor, who, in 1901, when she was sixty-three, climbed into a barrel and became the first person to go over Niagara Falls and survive.

"Now that old gal had *courage*," her grandmother marveled. She said "courage" like it was something rare and precious. Lorraine wanted that for her child. She wished she had more of it herself.

When Jerry finally did come home, it was a Tuesday night and he reeked of alcohol. Lorraine cradled the baby. She forced a smile.

"This is our new daughter, Jerry. Isn't she beautiful?"

He tilted his head.

"What're we gonna call her?"

"Annie."

Jerry snorted.

"Like the movie? What for?"

✍

From that moment on, Lorraine felt as if she were raising Annie by herself. Jerry took longer truck runs. He'd be gone for weeks. When he was home, he wanted his sleep undisturbed, his food on time, and his wife's full attention when he was ready to pay some to her. If Lorraine looked up at her daughter's crying, Jerry would grip her jaw and turn her face back towards him, saying, "Hey, I'm talking now."

His anger increased as the months passed. So did his physical force. Lorraine was ashamed at how afraid she'd become of him, and how quickly she responded to his demands, hoping to avoid his grabbing or pushing. They never went out. She was constantly washing clothes and dishes. There were times when she wondered how, in just a few years, her life had gone from so open to so shut. She often thought about a different path, if she hadn't worked at that bakery, hadn't met Jerry, hadn't gotten in his truck that night, hadn't been in such an impetuous rush to get married.

But then she'd scold herself for imagining a world without her daughter in it, and she would lift Annie and feel her small bulk lying against her and Annie's buttery cheeks and the way she slid her arms around Lorraine's neck, and it erased any thought of another life.

This is the disarming power of children: their need makes you forget your own.

❧

By Annie's third birthday, Lorraine sensed her marriage would not last. By Annie's fourth birthday she was sure of it. Jerry's absences were no longer just about work, and when she confronted him over other women, his violence erupted. Lorraine tolerated him out of misguided guilt and the belief that her little girl needed a father, no matter how bad he was.

But when Jerry took his anger out on Annie, slapping her again and again after Annie opened the freezer against his wishes, Lorraine found a strength she hadn't known. She threw him out. She changed the locks. She held Annie that night and cried into her curly hair, and Annie cried, too, although she didn't know why.

The divorce dragged on. Jerry claimed he wasn't working. Money became a struggle. Lorraine took on typing jobs from home. Knowing Annie was confused about her father's absence, Lorraine tried to create a happy world for her. She encouraged Annie to dance freely, to sing loudly; they ran through sprinklers together and played board games for hours. Lorraine let Annie try pink lipstick in front of the mirror and choose her favorite superhero as a Halloween costume. For many months, mother and daughter shared the same bed, and Lorraine put Annie to sleep at night with a lullaby.

But as time passed, with the bills unpaid, Lorraine needed to take an outside job. She asked neighbors to watch Annie after school and was exhausted by the time she got home. Annie started sleeping in her own room. Eventually, Lorraine was asked out by men at her new office and she quickly accepted, especially when they paid for a babysitter. She had a string of short relationships, none of them successful. She continued trying, hoping to change her life.

Then came the day at Ruby Pier, when she got her wish, but not the way she wanted.

In heaven, vision can be shared, and Annie, having tumbled into her mother's eyes, now found herself inside one of Lorraine's memories, sitting at a table in the backyard of their first home. The sky was white. A laundry pole had sheets and clothes hanging, as did other laundry poles in other yards.

Lorraine was wearing high heels with a blue skirt and a white blouse, an outfit she'd worn to work. There was a manila folder on her lap and documents in her hands.

"Do you know what these are, Annie?"

Annie, still trying to understand how they got here, shook her head no.

"They're from a lawyer. Your father had them sent."

Annie blinked. "Why?"

"He claimed I was an unfit mother. Because of your accident. He wanted custody."

"Of me?"

"Full-time."

"But I hadn't seen Dad—"

"In years. I know. But he wanted to sue the amusement park, and he needed you to do that. He thought he could get big money. And when Jerry got a money idea, he didn't give up.

"I knew what your life would be like if he took you. I knew how violent he was. So I made a decision."

Annie glanced at the bedroom window. She saw her younger self looking out.

"I remember this day . . . It was when those reporters came to the door."

"That's right."

"We left the next morning."

"I never told you why."

Lorraine laid down the papers.

"Now you know why."

She stood and flattened her skirt.

"So that's a start," she said.

"A start of what?" Annie asked.

"Of ending our secrets. Come. There's more to show you."

Annie felt herself floating beside her mother. They rose above the house. The afternoon sky melted to dawn, and Annie saw their car pulling away the next morning, its trunk held down by a bungee cord.

"I hated leaving," she said.

"I know you did."

"Things were never the same."

"They couldn't be."

"We walked away from everything."

"Well, not everything."

They dropped lower to see Lorraine behind the wheel, Annie asleep in the seat next to her.

"Not each other," Lorraine said.

Annie Makes a Mistake

She is fourteen. Paulo's family is about to move to Italy.

Annie has been dreading this day. She and Paulo eat lunch together now. They meet between classes. She has come to think of him as more than a friend, as someone to really like or, in her young way, to love. Not that she does anything about it. First loves often remain in the heart, like plants that cannot grow in sunlight.

But she pictures Paulo every day. She imagines them holding hands, nudging against each other at the zoo or the mall. Only now he is leaving and Annie isn't just losing her friend (and whatever else he has yet to become) but also her shield from the other girls in school.

The morning of Paulo's last day, Annie stands by her locker, retrieving her books. Megan, one of the popular girls who never talks to her, approaches and says, "Hey," and Annie, taken aback, says, "Hey," and Megan says, "I bet you're going to miss Paulo," and Annie blushes, but Megan says, "No, seriously. He's cute. I would miss him if he noticed me like he notices you."

Annie is surprised by her words and tone. She is swept up in the possibility of a new friend. Megan smiles and Annie has an urge to please her.

"Look," Annie says, flipping open a notebook. It is a pencil drawing she made of Paulo during classes when she was bored. Annie is a good artist and the rendering is large, with Paulo's eyes big and emphasized.

"Oh, my God, that is so good," Megan says. "I have to take a picture." She pulls out a small phone, and before Annie can object, she presses a button. Annie has never seen a phone that is a camera.

"It's new," Megan says, flipping it Annie's way. "So cool, right?"

She shows Annie other photos of her friends preening for the lens. Annie feels like she is inside a special circle.

The bell rings.

"Bye," Megan says.

Annie watches her rush off. Maybe Paulo's leaving won't be the end, she thinks. Maybe she can talk about him with Megan—and other things the popu-

lar girls talk about. It is a new feeling for Annie and she lets it wash over her, brightening her mood.

At the end of the school day, she walks towards Paulo's locker, where she usually meets him. She has a plan. They will talk like they normally do, maybe extra-long this time. She wants to give him the picture she drew. She wants to tell him to write from Italy and she will write back. Mostly she wants to kiss him. It wouldn't seem too weird, she figures, since he is leaving. People kiss, right? A peck on the cheek? Or maybe on the lips? She has been thinking about it all day. Actually, for many days.

She turns down the hallway.

She freezes.

A group of students is gathered around Paulo's locker. Paulo is in the middle. They are all laughing, girls and boys, and some of the boys are slapping Paulo on the back. Megan is in the middle. She is showing everyone her phone.

"Dude, it really looks like you!" a boy yells.

"She's your stalker!" yells another.

"She wants to wear your skin as a birthday present!"

Everyone laughs. Annie watches Paulo. He is not saying anything.

Suddenly, one of them spots Annie and says, "Whoa!" and they tap each other and turn her way. It's like being shot with arrows. She can barely swallow. She sees Megan tucking the phone behind her back.

Normally, Annie would duck and disappear. But something about Paulo standing in their midst. It's like they've taken the last thing she had. With her feet moving as if someone else were operating them, she edges forward, as the other kids peel back like reversed magnets. She is face-to-face with Megan.

Annie swallows hard.

"Can I see, too?" she asks.

Megan rolls her eyes. She holds up the phone. Annie sees the photo of her drawing. Paulo. His big eyes.

"Why would you show that to everybody?" Annie says, her voice shaking. "It's not yours."

She turns to Paulo. "It was supposed to be yours."

Paulo's mouth drops open. For a moment, all of them are frozen. Then, with Paulo inches away, something releases inside of Annie. It propels her forward. The next thing she knows, she is pressing her lips against his. It lasts a second. She feels tears leaving her eyes.

"Goodbye," she whispers.

She turns and walks away, fighting her impulse

to run. She hears one of the girls say, "Yeah, go on, geek." She hears someone else say, "Oh ... my ... God." When she turns the corner, she no longer holds back. She runs and keeps running, out the back doors and down the street, tears burning her cheeks.

She reaches a park and drops onto a bench, flanked by two blue garbage bins. She doesn't come home until dark. When she enters, her mother is livid.

"Why are you so late?" she yells.

"Because I felt like it!" Annie yells back.

Lorraine grounds her for a month.

The next day, Paulo is gone.

ALL CHILDREN KEEP SECRETS. All parents do the same. We mold the version we want others to believe, boosting the disguise and tucking away the truth. It is how we can be loved by our closest family members and still, at times, elude them.

From their hasty cross-country journey to their new roots in rural Arizona, Lorraine held her secrets close. She took great pains to erase her past. She got rid of old photos. She stopped calling old friends. She never mentioned her ex-husband. She never spoke of Ruby Pier.

She hoped a new state would mean a new life. But the things we have done are never far behind us. And like a shadow, they go where we do.

Annie, meanwhile, had given up on old hopes. By sixteen, she had accepted her role as a high school outcast. She had few friends and spent much of her time at home, reading, with her dog, Cleo, curled against her. Her figure had developed, and she sometimes caught boys staring if she wore tight clothing. Their attention confused her. Being noticed was all right, but she wanted to be known. They never even spoke to her.

One day, in history class, Annie's teacher was asking about family roots.

"What about you, Annie?"

Annie slid low in her seat. She hated being called upon. She glanced sideways and saw one of those boys with the juvenile stare.

"I don't know much," she said.

Another student sang those words, *"Don't know much,"* from a popular song, and the class laughed. Annie reddened.

"Well, you weren't born in Arizona, were you?"

"No," Annie admitted, breaking one of her mother's rules.

"Where did you begin?"

Trying to get this over with, Annie spat out a few details, the town, how many years, where she thought her grandparents came from.

"And why did you move here?" the teacher said.

Annie froze. She couldn't think of a lie. She heard someone snickering, "It's not a trick question."

"I had an accident," Annie mumbled.

An awkward silence.

"All right, who else?" the teacher said.

Annie exhaled.

Before the class ended, the teacher assigned the students to research world events on the day they were born. They could use the school library or, if they had access, computer search engines, which were new.

Annie didn't own a computer. She used the library microfilm. She learned that on her birthday, a crisis in South Africa ended and a famous hockey player broke a league record. She wrote it down.

At the end of the week, the students were asked to report their findings. Annie rose and recited her meager facts, then quickly sat, glad that it was over. She gazed out the window, drifting, until she heard Megan, the girl who had ruined everything with Paulo, ending her report by saying, "Also, I used a computer, and I found out that Annie's 'accident' was in an amusement park and that someone died because of her."

Students gasped. One yelled, "*What?*" Annie flushed with chills. She began to cough. She couldn't find her breath. Her mind was racing between the faces staring at her and that day at Ruby Pier, replaying fragments, the train ride, her mother taking off with Bob. She felt woozy. Her arm slid off the desk.

"Annie, are you all right?" the teacher said. "Come here, come here, let's go . . ."

She rushed Annie out the classroom door.

When Annie came home that day, she marched into the trailer, slammed her books on a table, and started screaming about what Megan said in class. Lorraine, hovering over a pile of bills, froze for a moment, a pen in her hand. Then she resumed scribbling, looking down through her reading glasses.

"You knew it was an amusement park," she said.

"What about the rest, Mom?"

"What?"

"Did I kill someone?"

"Of course not!" Lorraine capped the pen. "That's an evil lie by an evil girl."

"Are you sure?"

"How could you even think that?"

"Did someone die?"

"It was a big accident, Annie. There were work-ers. Operators. Riders. Lots of people were affected. You were a victim, remember? We could have sued. Maybe I should have. All these bills."

"Did someone *die*?"

"An employee, I think. No one that you knew."

"What else happened?"

Lorraine pulled off her glasses. "Do you really

need more details? Now, all of a sudden? Haven't we been through enough?"

"We?" Annie screamed. "Really, Mom? WE?"

"Yes!" Lorraine screamed back. "Really, Annie. WE!"

"I have *no friends*, Mom! I want to have friends!"

"I'd like some, too, Annie!"

"I'm never going back to that class!"

"You're never going back to that school!"

"Fine!"

"Fine!"

Both of them were red-faced and breathing hard. Lorraine rose to the kitchen. She smacked the faucet and rubbed her hands vigorously under the water. "Honestly, what kind of learning is that? Looking up your birthdays? You'd be better off home-schooled."

"I'm not doing THAT!" Annie yelled.

"We'll find someplace."

"Oh, God, Mom! GOD!"

Annie dropped on the couch. She pulled a pillow over her face.

Later that week, she transferred, and when she didn't like that school, she transferred to another. The matter of the accident was not spoken about again.

But just because you have silenced a memory does not mean you are free of it.

❧

The change in schools made Annie more determined to escape Lorraine's restrictions. By senior year, she found a way to circumvent them altogether.

A boyfriend with a car.

His name was Walt, a year older than Annie, with a lanky frame, a sharp nose, and triangular sideburns. Annie spent most of her evenings and weekends with him. He smoked hand-rolled cigarettes and liked grunge music. He found Annie curious ("You're weird, but in a good way," he said), which pleased her because it meant attention, including physical attention, the first she'd had from a boy.

Annie, by this point, had bloomed into her tall, shapely frame, with a wayward mop of long, curling hair and, as everyone seemed to point out, nice, straight teeth. She dressed in modest clothes, favoring leggings and beat-up sneakers. She finished high school with a grade point average of four and a friend count of two: Judy, who wore horn-rimmed glasses and vintage 1950s clothing, and Brian, a math whiz with a thin mustache that he was constantly fingering.

Annie didn't see either one of them after the graduation ceremony. She stayed only long enough to get her diploma and a handshake from the school's principal, who whispered, "Good luck, Annie. You can go places."

Annie did. She walked off the stage and went straight to the parking lot, where Walt was waiting by his green Nissan coupe.

"Yay, you're done," he deadpanned.

"Thank God," Annie said.

"Where do you want to go?"

"Anywhere."

"You need to call your mom?"

"I told her not to come. She probably came anyhow."

"She's still in the audience?"

"I guess."

Walt looked over her shoulder. "Guess again."

Annie turned to see her mother, in a turquoise skirt and blazer, a cloche hat on her head, wobbling across the school's front lawn, her high heels catching in the grass. She waved her arms and yelled, "Annie! What are you doing?" The wind was blowing and she grabbed her hat to hold it down.

"Let's go," Annie mumbled.

"You don't want to wait?"

"I said, let's go."

She got in the car and slammed the door shut. Walt started the engine. They drove off, leaving Lorraine, hand on her hat, watching them zoom past a sign that read CONGRATULATIONS, GRADUATES!

Annie didn't speak to her for a year.

During that time, Annie moved in with Walt, sharing the basement of his father's house, a small Craftsman bungalow an hour from the trailer park. Annie knew, being so far away, there was no chance of running into her mother, and she enjoyed the freedom that feeling provided. She chopped her hair in the front and dyed it purple. Walt gave her a T-shirt that read I OWE YOU NOTHING. She wore it often.

Walt's father worked nights at a creamery. Walt fixed cars at a nearby auto shop. Annie's grades got her a scholarship at a local community college, and she took English literature and photography classes, fancying herself one day taking pictures for a travel magazine. Maybe she would go to Italy and find where Paulo lived, show up with a camera and say, *"Oh, hey, what a coincidence."*

As the months passed, she thought about calling her mother, especially when Walt would act like a child, pouting over food, not wanting to shower before they went out. But, like many her age, Annie's thirst for independence overruled her need for guidance. Besides, who was her mother to talk about men? Annie couldn't bear what she knew she would hear: *"Is this really how you want to spend your life, Annie? In your boyfriend's basement?"* The thought of that made her put down the phone.

Then, the following summer, she stopped by the hospital to surprise her Uncle Dennis, who had moved his practice to Arizona a few years earlier. It was after five o'clock and no one was at the reception desk, so she walked back to his office and tapped on the door. She heard a muffled "Yes?" and turned the knob.

"Annie?" Dennis said, his eyes widening.

"Hi, I was in the—"

She stopped. Her throat tightened. Sitting in a chair, just inches away, was her mother. Her face was gaunt; her eyes were hollow. Beneath a blue sweater and tan slacks, her limbs were thinner than Annie had ever seen them, sickly thin, as if she'd been melted.

"Hello, sweetheart," Lorraine said weakly. She

glanced at her brother. "So you don't have to tell her after all."

❦

The cancer had attacked Lorraine quickly, and by six months it had spread past all known cures. Treatment, at this point, was more about comfort than healing.

Annie, stunned by the sudden turn, didn't know how to react. She felt guilty for being absent when it had happened, and obliged to give her mother whatever time she now could. A trip to the pharmacy. A coffee shop after work. Just like that, they were back in each other's orbits. But their conversations were less about what was said than what was not.

"How's your tea?" Annie would ask.

"It's fine," Lorraine would answer.

"How's school?" Lorraine would ask.

"It's fine," Annie would answer.

Neither had the strength to confront the emotions they shielded. They were polite. They pecked each other's cheeks. Annie held the car door open and braced her mother's arm as she walked. Perhaps if there had been more time, the wall between them would have crumbled.

But the world does not cater to our timing.

"I love you, Annie," Lorraine rasped one night, as Annie handed her a plate of stir-fried vegetables.

"Eat," Annie said. "You need your strength."

"Love is strength," Lorraine said.

Annie touched her mother's shoulder. She felt the sharpness of the bone as if the skin barely existed.

Two days later, Annie's cell phone woke her up before the alarm clock.

"You better come to the hospital," Dennis whispered.

He broke down crying, and Annie broke down, too.

The gathering at the cemetery was small, owing to the secrecy Lorraine had draped around their lives. Only Annie, Walt, Uncle Dennis, and a few work colleagues stood by the grave as a pastor recited a prayer.

"It's funny," Lorraine said now, as the scene appeared in front of them. "You always wonder about your funeral. How big? Who'll show up? In the end it's meaningless. You realize, once you die, that a funeral is for everyone else, not you."

They watched Annie, in a black dress, sobbing into her uncle's shoulder.

"You were so sad," Lorraine observed.

"Of course."

"Then why did you shut me out for so long?"

"I'm sorry, Mom."

"I know you're sorry. I'm asking you why?"

"You know why." Annie sighed. "You embarrassed me. You smothered me. Every social thing I wanted to do. Every chance to have fun. I felt like a prisoner in my own childhood.

"I couldn't make friends. I wasn't allowed to do anything. Everyone thought I was weird, the girl whose mother wouldn't let her go." Annie lifted her left hand. "This didn't help."

Lorraine looked off. The image of the cemetery faded from view.

"What do you really know about that day?"

"At Ruby Pier?"

"Yes."

"I don't know anything, remember? It's the big black hole of my life. You wouldn't talk about it, that's for sure. We went there on a train. We bought tickets. I woke up in the hospital, covered in bandages . . ."

Annie felt an old anger rising. She shook her head. What was the point of anger in heaven?

"Anyhow, that's what I know," she grumbled.

"Well, I know more," her mother said, taking Annie's hand. "And it's time I told you."

The Third Lesson

Suddenly, they were back at Ruby Pier, under a hot summer sun. In the foreground was a long, wide boardwalk, teeming with beachgoers. Parents pushed baby strollers. Joggers and skateboarders weaved through the crowd.

"Do I know these people?" Annie asked.

"Look below," her mother said.

Under the boardwalk, Annie saw her younger mother, walking in the sand with Bob, the man from the train. Lorraine was barefoot, holding her shoes. Bob kept pulling her towards him. Lorraine pushed away playfully. Then, at one point, she glanced at her watch and looked out towards the sea. Bob turned her chin back his way and kissed her mouth hard.

"Did you ever think about getting a moment back?" Lorraine asked, as she watched alongside her daughter. "A moment where you can't believe how unimportant what you were doing was, and how critical the thing you missed would be?"

Annie nodded.

"That was mine," her mother said. "At that moment, I was thinking of you. I remember, because my watch read 3:07. Your birthday. March seventh. I thought, 'I should get back to Annie.'"

"But you didn't."

"No," Lorraine said, softly. "I didn't."

They continued to watch Bob clutching at Lorraine, smacking kisses on her neck. He pulled her arm and they dropped to the sand.

"I made a lot of bad choices after your father left us," Lorraine said. "I felt unwanted, unattractive. I felt that being a single mother, men wouldn't be interested in me. So I overdid it. I chased one after another. I wanted to change my life."

Annie remembered a steady stream of her mother's paramours coming by after Annie's bedtime. She would sneak from her room and tuck around the top of the stairs, watching her mother leave with the latest man, as a babysitter shut the door.

"I was still young myself," Lorraine said. "I wanted a fresh start. I wanted things I didn't have with your father—security, affection. He chose other women over me, and I guess, deep down, I wanted to prove he was missing something.

"That," she said, "was foolish. Love is not revenge. It can't be thrown like a rock. And you can't create it to fix your problems. Forcing love is like picking a flower then insisting that it grow."

Beneath the boardwalk now, Bob stopped pawing Lorraine long enough to remove his jacket. He laid it down on the sand behind them. Annie noticed her younger mother cup her elbows, a sudden scared look upon her face.

"At that moment, it hit me," Lorraine said. "Your father had done the same thing years before when we were first together. A beach. His jacket. Lying down in the sand. That's how it all started.

"I realized I was doing the same foolish things I had done with him. Why did I think anything would turn out differently?"

She looked directly at Annie. "I'm sorry, sweetheart. I was so desperate to find someone new to love me, I forgot I already had the best person. You."

"Mom," Annie whispered, "I didn't know any of this."

Lorraine nodded. "I didn't know much of it myself—until that day."

She motioned back to the boardwalk. They saw Lorraine rise quickly, grabbing her shoes. Bob looked angry, pulling at Lorraine's legs until she broke free and ran. Bob smacked a fist into the sand, spraying it onto his pants.

"At that point, Annie, I just wanted to gather you up, take you home, buy you ice cream. I wanted to make you the happiest girl in the world.

"It was like a curtain had lifted. I could be done with all those men who weren't right for me, done with the stupid flirting phone calls. I was finally seeing things straight."

"What happened?" Annie asked.

Lorraine looked off. "Just because you see things straight doesn't mean you see them in time."

They watched young Lorraine hurry onto Ruby Pier. An ambulance sped past her, lights flashing. Police officers were barking into radios. Lorraine spun back and forth, confused, as crowds surged on the midway. She pushed against the tide of onlookers, past the bumper cars, past the teacup ride, through the food pavilion, all the while yelling, "Annie! . . . Annie!"

Finally, after an hour of fruitless search, Lorraine spotted a police officer talking to a park worker, a wiry young man whose shirt patch read DOMIN-GUEZ. They stood beside yellow barricade tape. The wiry man had tears in his eyes.

"Can you help me?" Lorraine interrupted. "I'm sorry. I know you're dealing with whatever's going on. But it's my daughter. I can't find her. I've looked everywhere. I'm worried."

The policeman shot a glance at Dominguez.

"What did she look like?" the officer asked.

Lorraine described Annie. The cutoff shorts. The lime green T-shirt with a duck on the front.

"Oh, my God," Dominguez whispered.

Annie watched the heavenly sky turn a dull red.

"That was the lowest moment of my life," her mother said. "When my daughter most needed me, I was with a man I didn't even care about.

"By the time I reached the hospital, they had already started operating. I had to ask what they were doing. Me. Your mother. Asking like an outsider. I cried so hard. Not just for your pain, Annie, but for my own humiliation.

"All those rules? All the limits and curfews I would put on you? It was all because of that day. I never wanted to make another mistake."

"It just made me hate you," Annie said, softly.

"No more than I hated myself. I didn't protect you. I left you alone. After that, I could never think of myself as a good mother again.

"I was so ashamed. It made me hard on you, when I was trying to be hard on me. We are blinded by our regrets, Annie. We don't realize who else we punish while we're punishing ourselves."

Annie thought for a moment. "Is that the lesson you're here to teach me?"

"No," Lorraine said, quietly. "That's me sharing my most painful secret."

Annie stared at her mother's young, unblemished face, which suggested a woman still in her twenties. She felt a surge of something that had yet to visit her in the afterlife: the need to confess.

"I have a secret, too," Annie said.

Annie Makes a Mistake

She is twenty. She is pregnant. An old woman entering the doctor's office holds the door for Annie as she leaves.

"You don't have to do that," Annie says.

"It's all right," the woman says.

Annie touches her belly. It happened without planning. She and Walt were still living in the basement, their relationship running on inertia, a lack of better options making it easier to continue than quit.

Then one day, feeling unusually fatigued, Annie went to the campus clinic. She thought she had the flu. They took a blood test. The next day she went back.

"Well, it's not the flu," a doctor began.

She spent the rest of the day hiding in the library, one hand on her stomach, the other clutching a tissue. Pregnant? she thought. She felt too depressed to move. Only when a janitor nudged her to say, "We're closing," did she rise and drag herself home.

The talk with Walt was less than satisfying. Af-

ter laughing nervously, then unleashing a stream of curses, he stomped up and down the steps for half an hour. He finally agreed to marry Annie for the sake of the child.

"Before I start showing," Annie insisted.

"Yeah, all right," Walt said.

The next month, they went to a courthouse (as Lorraine and Jerry had done decades earlier) and signed some papers. Two weeks later, they made it official.

Walt told his father.

Annie told no one.

Like her mother, Annie was facing unintended parenthood. Like her mother, she had a husband who was less than enthused. At times, Annie wished Lorraine were still alive. She wanted to ask her what to expect. But most of the time, she was glad her mother wasn't there to see this. Annie couldn't bear the disappointment. Certainly not the "Didn't I warn you to be careful?" that she knew she would hear. Annie had become the embodiment of all of her mother's phobias, a foolish daughter who wasn't mindful enough and now had the obstetrician's phone number on a sticky note in her father-in-law's basement.

Walt became docile, like a scolded puppy. He said little when he came home at night, opting instead to watch hours of television, his body slumped so deeply into the couch he resembled another cushion. Annie did not react. What was the point? She had come to believe that living with a man was more about tolerance than romance, and marriage was just another letdown along the way.

Now, back at the doctor's office, the old woman holding the door gives Annie a smile.

"How far along?"

"Seven months."

"Won't be long now."

Annie nods.

"Well, good luck," the woman says.

Annie walks away. She hasn't felt luck in a very long time.

That night, Annie skips dinner. She decides to assemble a plastic bookcase from IKEA. As she twists, Annie feels a sharp pain in her abdomen. It doubles her over.

"Oh, no . . ." she moans. "No . . . no . . . Walt!"

Walt races her to the hospital. He leaves the car by the emergency entrance. The next thing Annie knows, she is on a gurney, rolling through a hallway.

The baby comes just after midnight: a tiny boy,

weighing less than three pounds. Annie doesn't see him until hours later, inside an incubator in the neonatal intensive care unit. The premature birth means the child's lungs have not fully developed. "We need to help him breathe," a doctor says.

Annie sits in a blue hospital gown, staring at the incubator. Is she really a mother now? She can't even touch her child. There are tubes to feed and medicate him, white tape that crosses his pinkish cheeks to hold a breathing device in place, and an oh-so-small blue cap over his head and ears, to keep him warm. Annie feels locked out. The apparatus is handling everything.

As day turns to night and night again to day, she sits, unmoving, through a parade of doctors, nurses, and hospital staff.

"Do you want to call anyone?" a nurse asks.

"No."

"Do you want some coffee?"

"No."

"Do you want to take a break?"

"No."

What she wants to do, more than anything, is reach under the dome and grab this tiny creature and run. She thinks about her mother and the time they packed up and disappeared.

Then, at 10:23 a.m., a monitor begins to beep, and a nurse enters, followed by another nurse, followed by a doctor. Within minutes, the incubator is being rushed out to surgery. Annie is told to wait.

The baby never returns.

Three days after his birth, the tiny boy dies. The doctors are grim-faced, insisting they did their best. The nurses whisper, "This is the hardest thing." Annie remains stoic, gazing blankly at their sympathy and the now-empty room. She listens to Walt repeatedly mumble, "Oh, man, I can't believe it." She studies the windows and the floor and the metal sinks. She stares at inanimate objects as if boring a hole with her eyes, until hours later, when a social worker, holding a clipboard, approaches gingerly about some information needed for "the paperwork"—the paperwork meaning a death certificate.

"What was the child's name?" she begins.

Annie blinks. She hadn't chosen a name. The question feels like the hardest quiz in the world. A name. A name? For some reason, the only name she can think of is her mother's, Lorraine, and her mouth spits out something close.

"Laurence," she mumbles.

"Laurence," the nurse repeats.

Laurence, Annie thinks. The word hits her like a

sudden spray of water. Once the baby has a name, he is real. And once he is real, he is really gone.

"Laurence?" Annie whispers, as if asking for him. She breaks down sobbing and doesn't speak for days.

WHEN ANNIE FINISHED telling her story, she realized she was weeping as she had wept back in that hospital. As her tears hit the ground, they created a pool that swelled into a stream, which swelled into a river, turquoise in shade, clear to the bottom. Trees appeared on the riverbank, with wide, colorful leaves that spread open like umbrellas.

"You've been waiting a long time to share that with me," Lorraine said.

"Forever," Annie whispered.

"I know. I felt it."

"Here?"

"Even here."

"I never told anyone except Uncle Dennis. I never even told Paulo. I couldn't."

Lorraine looked to the trees.

"Secrets. We think by keeping them, we're controlling things, but all the while, they're controlling us."

"The baby couldn't breathe," Annie said. "After the balloon crash, when they told me Paulo couldn't breathe, I was living it all over again. I said what I wanted to say back then: 'Take my lungs. Let me breathe for him. Just save his life.'"

Annie turned with a pleading expression.

"Mom. Did Paulo live? Just tell me. Please. If anyone can, you can, right?"

Lorraine touched her cheek. "It's not for me to know."

They were quiet for a while. Lorraine dipped her hand in the river water.

"Did I ever tell you why I named you Annie?"

Annie shook her head.

"A woman who went over Niagara Falls in a barrel. She was sixty-three. A widow. She was looking to make a name, to earn money for her old age. My grandmother used to say, 'That old gal had *courage*.' That's what I wanted for you. Courage."

Annie frowned. "I guess I didn't live up to my billing, huh?"

Lorraine raised her eyebrows. "Oh, but you did."

"Mom, please. I was the opposite of courage. I ran away. I lived in a basement. I got married for the wrong reason, had a child too soon, and couldn't even do that right. I was useless for a long time."

Her mother crossed her arms.

"And then?"

&

And then, the truth was, Annie found her footing. Her marriage to Walt was annulled after Walt claimed he was coerced by the pregnancy. Papers were signed. Walt asked for his sweatpants back.

Annie moved in with her Uncle Dennis. She stayed indoors for the first few months, lying in bed during the daylight hours. She mourned her baby. She mourned her mother. She mourned her lack of imagination about the future. What purpose could make her leave this room? Every idea seemed small, inconsequential. She was broken open.

But broken open is still open.

Winter turned to spring and spring approached summer. Annie began to get up earlier. From the window of her bedroom, she saw her uncle leaving for the hospital. She remembered when he first moved to Arizona; Annie was in junior high. She asked him why he left the East, where he had grown up. He said, "Your mother is my family." Annie had wanted to say, "You're kidding, right? You moved here for *her*?" But now she was glad he had. Who else would she have turned to?

At night, she heard her uncle talking to patients on the phone. He'd answer their questions calmly. Often, at the end, he would say, "That's what I'm here for." That made Annie proud. He was a good and decent man, and her admiration for him grew. In time, a seed took root in her mind. *That's what I'm here for.*

One evening, she came down to the kitchen, where Dennis was watching a football game on a small TV.

"Hey," he said, clicking off the set.

"Can I ask you something?" Annie said.

"Sure."

"How hard is it to be a nurse?"

∽

In the blue river of the afterlife, Lorraine cupped her hands and lifted water up, watching it pour through her fingers.

"This is your heaven?" Annie asked.

"Isn't it beautiful? I wanted serenity, after all the conflict of my life. Here I enjoy a calm I never knew on earth."

"And you've been waiting for me all this time?"

"What's time between a mother and her daughter? Never too much, never enough."

"Mom?"

"Yes?"

"We fought a lot."

"I know." She took Annie's left hand and guided it into the water. "But is that all you remember?"

Annie felt her fingers floating and her mind doing the same. In the water's reflection she saw only loving scenes from her childhood, countless memories, her mother kissing her good night, unwrapping a new toy, plopping whipped cream onto pancakes, putting Annie on her first bicycle, stitching a ripped dress, sharing a tube of lipstick, pushing a button to Annie's favorite radio station. It was as if someone unlocked a vault and all these fond recollections could be examined at once.

"Why didn't I feel this before?" she whispered.

"Because we embrace our scars more than our healing," Lorraine said. "We can recall the exact day we got hurt, but who remembers the day the wound was gone?

"From the moment you woke up in that hospital, I was different with you, and you were different with me. You were sullen. You were mad. You fought with me constantly. You hated my restrictions. But that wasn't the real reason for your anger, was it?"

Lorraine reached down and clutched Annie's fingers.

"Can you break that last secret? Can you say the real reason for your resentment since Ruby Pier?"

Annie choked up. Her voice was barely a whisper.

"Because you weren't there to save me."

Lorraine closed her eyes. "That's right. Can you forgive me for that?"

"Mom."

"Yes?"

"You don't need to hear me say it."

"No, I don't," Lorraine said, softly. "But you do."

Annie began to cry again, tears of release, blessed release, the expulsion of secrets bottled up for years. She realized the sacrifices Lorraine had made before and after that day at Ruby Pier, ending her marriage, giving up her home, forsaking her friends, her history, her desires, making Annie her only priority. She thought about her mother's small funeral, and how much of Lorraine's life had been surrendered to protect Annie's.

"Yes, yes, I forgive you, Mom. Of course I forgive you. I didn't know. I love you."

Lorraine placed her hands together.

"Grace?"

"Grace."

"*That*," Lorraine said, smiling, "is what I was here to teach you."

With that, Lorraine lifted off the ground and hovered above Annie, just for a moment. Then, with a final touch of her daughter's chin, she swelled back into the sky, until her face commanded the firmament once more.

"It's time to go, angel."

"No! Mom!"

"You need to make your peace."

"But we made our peace!"

"There's someone else."

Before Annie could respond, the river rushed and heavy rains began to fall. Annie was blown sideways, all but blinded by the downpour. She felt a sudden bump on her hip. A large wooden barrel was nudging against her. She tilted its top and pulled herself safely inside. The walls were stained with a brown substance, and there were pillows all around for cushioning, old pillows that Annie guessed were from the time her namesake made her famous passage. Annie jostled to a sitting position, feeling the river rumbling beneath her.

Then, with a jerk, the barrel surged ahead.

She heard the storm and water crashing against rocks, louder by the second, turning ominous, thunderous. She felt something she had yet to feel in heaven: pure fear. The barrel shot over a massive waterfall, out into a moment of such thick, violent noise, it was as if God's own voice were howling. In that rush, with nothing beneath her, Annie experienced the utter abandon of a free fall. She was helpless, beyond all control.

As she pushed against the walls, she looked up through a spray of white water and saw her mother's face gazing down, whispering a single word.

"Courage."

SUNDAY, 2:14 P.M.

Tolbert stepped away from the police officers, walked to the side of their car, and vomited.

He had just seen a carnage that would stay in his mind forever. The green spacious field was scarred with burned patches. At its center lay a passenger basket, charred beyond recognition. Scattered about, in dark, torn ribbons, were the only remains of Tolbert's once-majestic balloon.

An eyewitness to the crash, a male jogger wearing a yellow Reebok T-shirt, had given an account to the police: "The balloon hit something in those trees and I saw a flash of fire. It came down and hit the ground and shot back up. One person fell out. One was thrown out. I guess the last one jumped. Then the whole thing burst into flames."

The jogger had taken video with his cell phone and had called 9-1-1. All three passengers, two men, one woman, were rushed to the university hospital.

Tolbert's shock wrestled with his anger. He couldn't figure where these two customers had come from. It was so early. There had been no reservations. *What was Teddy doing? I was only gone for a few hours.*

He ran his palms over his face several times, then walked back to the police.

"If you're done with me here, I need to get to that hospital," he said.

"I'll drive you over," an officer said.

"All right."

Tolbert got in the squad car and pushed back into the seat, still grappling with this Sunday-morning tragedy, unaware of the part he had played in it.

The Next Eternity

The wooden barrel crashed the water's surface and dropped in quiet submersion. Annie yanked herself through the opening into a vast greenish deep; it seemed more like a sea than the base of a waterfall. She windmilled her arms and spun her head, her hair swirling around her like tentacles. Up above, she saw a circle of light, like the fat end of a telescope. She swam towards it.

When Annie broke the surface, her skin was instantly dry. The waters pulled back, and she found herself standing on the shore of a great gray ocean, wearing cutoff shorts and a lime green T-shirt that covered her hollow middle. The sky was a summer blue, lit to perfection—not by the sun, but by a single white star.

Annie felt the sand beneath her feet and a soft breeze on her cheeks. As she moved up the beach a magnificent pier came into view, with gilded towers, spires, domes, a wooden roller coaster, and a parachute drop.

It was an old amusement park, like the one Annie used to visit. It made her think about her mother. They had finally reconciled. A great weight had been lifted. Then she was gone. It felt so unfair. What was the point of heaven and its march of five people if each of them abandoned you just when solace was within reach?

"*You need to make your peace,*" her mother had said. Why? With whom? Annie just wanted things to stop. She felt drained, weary, like at the end of a long, hard day.

She took a half step and tripped over something in the sand. Looking down, she saw a stone marker. As the seawater rolled over it, two words were revealed:

EDDIE

MAINTENANCE

"Hey, kid," a gruff voice said, "you mind not standing on my grave?"

Annie Makes a Mistake

*She is twenty-five and working in a hospital clinic.
Uncle Dennis helped pay for nursing school, and
Annie, to her surprise, finds the field a good fit. She
always did well in science, so the medical study was
painless. But her composure with patients is a revela-
tion. She listens attentively. She pats their hands. She
grins at their jokes and shows compassion for their
complaints. Part of this stems from a childhood of
seeking intimacy that never came. As a nurse, she is
actually sought out by patients for attention, comfort, even counsel. She finds herself pleased to give it.*

*Her supervisor, Beatrice, is a stout Southern
woman who wears bright red lipstick and sleeveless
blouses, even in winter. She has an easy sense of hu-
mor and compliments Annie on her work.*

"Patients trust you," she says. "That's a big deal."

*Annie likes Beatrice. Sometimes they stay late,
talking in the break room. One night, the issue of
repressed memory comes up. Annie asks if Beatrice
believes in that and Beatrice says she does.*

"People do all kinds of things because of stuff they don't remember," she says. "Half my relatives, if you ask me."

Annie decides to hint at her own childhood trauma.

"Something happened when I was eight."

"Oh, yeah?"

"An accident. A serious one. That's where I got this."

She shows Beatrice her scarred hand.

"Does it still bother you?"

"When it's cold. And if I don't move the fingers—"

"I meant whatever happened."

"Well, that's the thing. I don't know what happened. I blocked it out."

Beatrice thinks for a moment. "There are people you can talk to about that."

"Yeah, but . . ." Annie bites her lip.

"What?"

"There's something else."

"What?"

"I think someone got killed."

Beatrice's eyes widen. "Well, that's a story."

"If I talked to someone—"

"You're afraid of what you'd find out?"

Annie nods.

"*Honey, that may be why your head blocked it in the first place.*"

Beatrice puts a palm over Annie's bad hand.

"*When you're ready to remember, you'll remember.*"

Annie pushes up a smile. But she wonders if Beatrice will think less of her now, a woman with a secret she won't let herself see.

The Fourth Person Annie
Meets in Heaven

"It ain't *really* my grave."

Annie spun to see a squat old man standing in the sand, arms folded like flippers across his chest. He wore a pale brown uniform and a linen cap. The man from her wedding. The one she'd kept seeing.

"I did die here," he said. "Well, over there, in the park. The guys I worked with made that marker for my birthday. I used to call 'em 'brickheads,' so they gave me that brick. Buncha jokers."

He shrugged his thick shoulders. His hair was white, his ears were large, and his nose was flat with a crooked bridge, as if it had been broken more than once. The lines by his eyes cracked down to whiskered cheeks. They lifted now into a friendly grin.

"Hey, kiddo," he said, as if he knew her.

"You were at my wedding," Annie whispered. "You waved at me."

"I was kinda hoping you'd be older."

"Older?"

"You're awful young to be here."

"There was an accident."

She looked away.

"You can tell me," he said.

"A balloon. It caught fire. My husband and I were in it."

"And?"

"He was hurt. Really badly. He couldn't breathe."

"What about you?"

"They took one of my lungs. To save him. During the transplant, I must have . . ."

The old man raised an eyebrow.

"Died?"

Annie still winced at the word. "Yes. And I don't know what happened to my husband. All I remember is the operating room, a doctor touching my shoulders, saying, 'See you in a little bit.' Like I'd wake up in a few hours. But I never did."

"Lemme guess," the old man said, rubbing his chin. "You been asking everyone in heaven, 'Did my husband live? Did I save him?'"

"How did you know?"

"Because when I first got here, I met five people, too. And with every one of them, before I was through, I asked the same question, 'cause I couldn't remember my last seconds on earth. 'What happened? Did I save the little girl? Was my life a big waste?'"

"Wait," Annie said. "The little girl?"

The old man set his gaze and Annie felt powerless to turn away. She locked on a cloth patch near his heart, stitched with the same two words from the beach marker.

"'Eddie . . . Maintenance,'" she said.

"Little girl," he answered back.

He held out his beefy fingers, and Annie's lifted to meet them involuntarily. When they made contact, she felt safer than she'd ever felt before, like a baby bird crawling beneath the shelter of a mighty wing.

"It's all right, kiddo," the old man whispered. "It's all gonna clear up now."

∽

When people suffer a near-death experience, they often say, "My whole life flashed before my eyes." Scientists have even studied this phenomenon, aware that certain brain cortices can suffer hypoxia and blood loss, which, during a great trauma, might trigger a release of memories.

But science only knows what it knows. And because it lacks an understanding of the next world, it cannot explain that the flash before your eyes is actually a peek behind the curtain of heaven, where your life and the lives of all you've touched are on the same plane, so that seeing one memory is the same as seeing them all.

On the day of Annie's accident, at the moment of her greatest danger, Eddie, the maintenance man at Ruby Pier, made a split-second decision: to dive across the platform of Freddy's Free Fall and shove Annie away from a falling cart. What flashed before his eyes, just before his death, was every interaction he'd had on earth.

Now, here in heaven, with her fingers pressed against his, Annie saw them, too.

ℐ

She saw an infant Eddie born into poverty in the early 1920s. She saw a sparkle in his mother's eyes, and frequent beatings from his drunken father.

She saw a school-aged Eddie playing catch with

the sideshow workers at Ruby Pier. She saw a teen-aged Eddie fixing rides beside his old man. She saw Eddie bored and dreaming of a different life. She saw his father say, "Whatsa matter? Ain't this good enough for ya?"

She saw the night Eddie met his one true love—a girl in a yellow dress whose name was Marguerite—and how they danced to a big band at the Stardust Band Shell. She saw their romance interrupted by war, and Eddie sent to combat in the Philippines.

She saw his platoon captured and tortured in a prison camp. She saw a daring revolt, and the killing of their tormentors. She saw Eddie burning down the huts where they'd been imprisoned. She saw him shot in the leg during their escape. She saw his return to peacetime hobbled by wounds and dark memories.

She saw Eddie and Marguerite married and settled, deeply in love, but childless. And, upon his father's death, she saw Eddie forced to take over the maintenance job at Ruby Pier. She saw him sitting down in his life, depressed that after years of trying to break away, he was no different than his old man, "a nobody who never done nothing," he would say.

She saw Marguerite, in her late forties, die from a brain tumor, and Eddie go hollow with grief. She saw him hide inside his work, crying where no one could see him, inside darkened fun houses or underneath a water slide.

She saw Eddie visit the cemetery dutifully, through his sixties, his seventies, into his eighties, leaving flowers at Marguerite's grave, riding home in the front of the taxi to feel less lonely.

And she saw the final day of Eddie's life, his eighty-third birthday, when he checked a fishing line and inspected a roller coaster and sat in a beach chair and fashioned a rabbit made of yellow pipe cleaners. Which he handed to a little girl.

A little girl named Annie.

"Thaaaank you," she squealed, dancing off.

The image froze.

"That," Eddie said now, holding Annie's grip, "was the last thing you said to me on earth."

"What happened next?" she asked.

He let go of her hand. The image disappeared.

"Let's walk," he said.

The ocean pulled back, as if clearing a path, and they moved along the shore. The lone star in the blue firmament lit their way. Eddie told Annie about his own journey to heaven. He told her he, too, met five people, including a sideshow worker whose skin was blue, his old army captain, and the original Ruby of Ruby Pier. By the time he was finished, nearly everything he thought about his life had changed.

Then Eddie asked about Annie's existence, saying he'd often wondered what she'd done with the years. Feeling safe in his company, Annie spoke of many things. She spoke of her early childhood, which she remembered one way, fun and carefree, and her life after the accident, which was different.

"What changed?"

"Everything." She held up her hand. "Starting with this."

Eddie took her wrist in his meaty palm. He studied the scars as if discovering a lost map.

"After that," Annie said, "everything I tried went wrong. I couldn't make friends. I was at war with my mother. I had an awful first marriage. I lost . . ."

Eddie glanced up.

"I lost a child. I suffered depression. I gave up on ever being happy until I saw Paulo again. I thought he was my chance. I knew him. I trusted him. I loved him."

She paused. "Love him."

Eddie let go of her wrist. He seemed to be thinking of something.

"Would you change it back? Your hand? If you could?"

Annie stared at him. "That's so strange. Paulo asked me the same thing when we were kids."

"What did you say?"

"What I'd say now. Of course. Who would want to go through this if they didn't have to?"

Eddie nodded slowly, but Annie wasn't sure he agreed with her.

"Is your wife here?" Annie asked.

"She's not part of your journey."

"But you get to be with her? In your heaven?"

Eddie smiled. "It wouldn't be my heaven without her."

Annie tried to smile back, but hearing this made her feel worse. Her biggest desire was that Paulo had survived, that his life had been spared by the transplant. But that meant being alone now in the afterlife. Would Paulo move on without her on earth? Find someone else? By the time he died, would he choose a different heaven, one that didn't include Annie?

"What is it?" Eddie said. "You don't look so hot."

"It's just . . . I ruin everything," Annie said. "Even the good things. Even my wedding night. It was my idea to help a man on the highway. My pushing to go for a balloon ride."

She looked down. "I make so many mistakes."

Eddie glanced to the single star gleaming above them.

"I used to think the same thing," he said.

Suddenly, day changed to night. The air grew hot and sticky. The landscape turned barren. On naked hills around them, small fires erupted. Annie felt the ground thicken by their feet.

"What's happening?" she asked.

"We ain't done yet," Eddie said.

Annie Makes a Mistake

She is twenty-eight. It's been eight years since the baby's death. Today is the anniversary. She switches to an afternoon shift at the hospital and, after the morning rush hour, drives to the cemetery.

It is misty and damp. As she walks to the grave, she hears the gravelly drag of her feet. When she reaches the marker, she steps on the grass, lightly, as if not to disturb things. She reads Laurence's name and the etched dates that declare his brief time on earth:

FEBRUARY 4—FEBRUARY 7

The dash in between seems a truer measure.

"I wish I knew how to pray better," she whispers. "I wish I knew what to ask for you."

For the millionth time, she tells herself she wasn't really a mother, she never changed a diaper, never held a bottle, never rocked her son to sleep. She feels almost foolish, locked out of the very identity she is grieving.

The traffic is heavy going back to the hospital. She is agitated from the visit, and reaches into her purse for an anti-anxiety pill. Normally she takes these at night, but she reminds herself she has a whole shift to go, and she'd like to get through it with minimal drama. Besides, if this day doesn't call for some relief, what does?

"Guess what?" a fellow nurse says when she arrives. "Terry called in sick."

"No one is covering?"

"Nope. It's you and me."

The next six hours are rushed, covering multiple rooms. Annie doesn't sit once. The call lights keep flicking on, and the two nurses scramble to deal with them. Annie grabs plastic pouches of medications earmarked for each patient and fastidiously administers them, working her way down the hall.

When she reaches room 209K/L the patient on the right is sleeping, a thin, older man connected to a feeding tube. Annie finds the pill crusher and opens the medication pouch, preparing to administer it by syringe.

"Nurse, I need help here," the man in the next bed yells. He is bald and heavyset, his belly lifting the sheet. "I can't get comfortable on this pillow."

"I'll be right there," Annie says.

"I can't sleep with this pillow."

"Just a second."

"Can you get me another pillow?"

Annie keeps crushing the medicine. She gets the purified water to dissolve it.

"I need to sleep," the man whines.

Annie exhales. She presses the call button, hoping the other nurse will come, but she knows the buttons have been lit all afternoon.

"Come on," the large man says.

"I'll be right there."

"Damn it! That guy can wait! He's out cold!"

Annie is half shaking from the man's screaming and half dragging from the medication she took. She rubs her forehead and pulls her eyebrows together, as if squeezing out a headache, then swishes the crushed pill in the water and takes it up with the syringe.

"My neck is so stiff," the man moans.

Annie places the syringe in the tube port. She fastens the tip tightly and fingers the clasp to allow the medicine to flow into the patient's body.

"COME ON, NURSE!"

Of all the days, Annie thinks, avoiding the man by staring at the pouch's medical label. She blinks. Something's wrong. The date on the pouch. It's not today. Of all the days. Today's date she knows, February 7, the anniversary of the worst thing that ever happened to her. The date on the label is Febru-

ary 3. As she opens the clasp, her brain races through an equation. Four days. What could change in four days? She sees a notation on the label, ER, *meaning "extended release"—a pill you would swallow, never crush. But this man can't swallow anymore. Maybe he could when they wrote this up—*

She jerks the syringe out of the port.

"Damn it, Nurse, this pillow is—"

"SHUT UP! JUST SHUT UP!"

Annie doesn't hear the words she just screamed. Her mind is fixated on what she almost did: inject time-release pain narcotics into a feeding tube— which would have administered the entire drug at once, a drug meant to release over twelve hours. She could have seriously harmed the sleeping man. She might have killed him.

"You can't tell a patient to shut up!" the fat man yells. "I'm going to report you. I'm going to make sure you—"

Annie can't hear him. Her breath fills her ears. She can feel her heartbeat nearly burst through her ribs. She grabs the syringe and the used plastic pouch, and she runs down the hall and whips them into the bin, feeling like a criminal trying to hide the telltale weapon.

She takes a two-week leave of absence, even though the hospital doesn't ask for it. When she returns, she vows a tighter focus than ever on her patients. No distractions. No personal issues. Do one thing right, Annie, she tells herself. One thing right.

The Fourth Lesson

The ground beneath Eddie and Annie turned muddy and wet. There were oil barrels up a hill and bamboo huts burning everywhere.

"What is this place?"

"War."

"When? Where?"

Eddie sighed. "War is the same every when and where."

He stepped forward, feet squishing. "This is the Philippines. World War II."

"You were a prisoner."

"Yeah."

"You escaped."

"Eventually."

"I saw this when you held my hands. You burned these huts."

"That's right," he said. "I did."

He trudged through the muck and found the remains of a primitive flamethrower, a long hose attached to a gasoline-tank backpack.

"I was afraid when I was captured. Scared outta my mind. When I got free, I let it out. We all did. We attacked. We destroyed. We burned this place to the ground. I thought I was justified. Maybe even brave. But I was doing something awful, something I never knew."

He motioned towards a hut and Annie saw a shadow running through the flames.

"Wait . . . Was that a *person*?"

Eddie looked down, as if he could not watch. Slowly, from the blaze, a young girl emerged, with a cinnamon complexion and hair the color of plums. She was on fire, flames licking off her. She stepped next to Eddie and the flames sizzled out, leaving her face and skin terribly burned. She put her hand in his.

"This is Tala," Eddie said, quietly. "She was hiding in that hut when I lit it up."

He fixed his gaze on Annie.

"She's in heaven," Eddie said, "because of me."

≈

Annie stepped back. A shot of fear ran through her, as if she'd been wrong about this old man, that his aura of safety was a ruse.

"Mistakes," Eddie declared. "That's what I'm here to teach you about. You felt like you kept making them? You feel like maybe you made one now?"

Annie looked away.

"I used to think the same thing," Eddie continued. "I thought my whole life was a mistake. Things kept happening to me, lousy things, until I finally gave up trying."

He shrugged. "I never even knew the worst mistake I made."

He turned to the little girl. He touched her hair, which hung in patches.

"Tala was hiding in that hut. I only learned that after I died. She met me in heaven. Said I burned her to death."

He bit his lip.

"It damn near killed me all over again."

"Why are you telling me this?" Annie asked.

Eddie walked Tala over to Annie, close enough to see the blisters on Tala's burned skin.

"You've been haunted by something most of your life, right? Something you can't remember, but it makes you feel bad about yourself?"

"How do you know that?" Annie asked, softly.

"Because my whole life, I did, too. I felt out of place. Like I was trapped at Ruby Pier and wasn't supposed to be there. Fixing rides? Who wants a lousy job like that? It had to be a mistake to ever take it, I thought.

"Then I died. And Tala explained why I was there. To protect kids, the thing I didn't do with her. She told me I was right where I was supposed to be."

He put his hand on the little girl's shoulder.

"And then she told me one more thing, something that took away my pain forever. My salvation, I guess, to use a fancy word."

"What did she say?"

Eddie smiled.

"That I died saving you."

∽

Annie began to tremble. Eddie took her hands.

"Go on. You can see it now."

"I can't."

"Yes, you can."

"I don't remember."

"You do."

She moaned softly. "I don't *want* to."

"I know. But it's time."

The sky went red, a fiery shade, and Annie felt her head jerk upwards, as if someone had yanked her hair; she was back to that day at Ruby Pier, looking up at her impending death. She saw a giant cart tilting at the top of Freddy's Free Fall. She saw riders being frantically pulled to safety. She saw people pointing and covering their mouths. She saw Eddie pushing through them, yelling instructions to clear out, to run. She saw people pushing and shoving in one direction and she saw herself run the other way, to an empty platform, crawling onto it and curling into a ball. She saw her body shaking. She saw herself mumbling, "Ma . . . Ma . . . Ma . . ."

She saw Eddie running towards her, his face contorted. She saw the massive black cart dropping like a bomb. She saw Eddie lunging, arms out. His big hands impacted her chest, pushing her backwards. She fell off the ledge, her bottom first, then the back of her legs, then her heels. Just as she lost contact, she glimpsed Eddie's body flat on the platform.

The cart crushed him like a boot crushing a bug.

Then something smaller came flying at Annie, so fast there wasn't time to blink. It chopped her wrist and she screamed louder than she'd ever screamed and her eyes closed and all details vanished, as if that dropping bomb had blown up everything, Annie, Eddie, the day, life itself.

⁓

"Oh, God, that's what happened," Annie groaned, as if waking from a dream. "I remember now. You pushed me. You saved my life. That piece chopped off my hand and I blacked out."

"Things get pretty clear up here," Eddie said.

Annie's mouth fell open and her eyes darted back and forth. She replayed the scene in her head.

"But . . ."

She let go of Eddie's grip. Her voice dropped.

"Then I did kill you."

"A cart killed me."

"It was my fault."

"A cable's fault."

"I blocked it out."

"You weren't ready."

"For what?"

"The truth."

"That you died?"

"There's more to truth than that."

He stepped away, his work boots squishing the soft ground. "On earth, we get the what of things. The why takes a little longer."

"No," Annie insisted. "There was no why! There was just me being where I shouldn't have been. And people covering it up. Nobody told me. I couldn't remember, and my mother kept it secret."

"She was protecting you."

"From what?"

"From what you're doing now—blaming yourself."

"I heard a rumor. In high school."

"And?"

Annie hesitated.

"I pretended like it didn't happen. I switched schools. To be honest . . ."

She cupped her elbows and pulled them in.

"I was glad I didn't remember."

She couldn't look at Eddie. "You gave your life for me," she whispered. "You sacrificed everything. And I couldn't even face the truth."

Annie dropped to the ground, her knees smacking the mud. "I'm so sorry. If only I had run the other way. Then you wouldn't have had to save me."

"You're not getting it," Eddie gently replied. "I *needed* to save you. It let me make up for the life I took.

"That's how salvation works. The wrongs we do open doors to do right."

⦿

Tala took Eddie's hand and rubbed it over her face and arms. The mottled scabs fell off. The singed skin peeled away. Her complexion was now perfect. She pushed five fingers into Eddie's belly.

"Tala was my fifth person. You're my next."

"Your next?" Annie said.

"You meet five people, then you're one of five for someone else. That's how heaven connects everybody."

Annie looked down. "My third person said I needed to make peace with you."

"Who was that?"

"My mother."

"Well, she was right about making peace," he said. "But she didn't mean me. You only have peace when you make it with yourself. I had to learn that the hard way."

He glanced at Tala.

"The truth is, I spent years thinking I was doing nothing 'cause I was a nobody. You spent years doing lots of things and thinking they were all mistakes."

He exhaled. "We were both wrong."

He leaned over and helped Annie to her feet.

"Hey, kiddo?"

She looked up.

"There's no such thing as a nobody. And there are no mistakes."

With that, the landscape melted as if running down a drain. The darkness of war faded. Tala, whose Filipino name means "star," lifted into the firmament, becoming the illumination for a perfect blue sky around them.

Annie felt herself rising, too, then dropping softly into the seat of a steel-rimmed Ferris wheel, rotating high above the sprawl of Ruby Pier. She gazed down on its colorful tents and rides. As she descended, the ground began to spark with tiny lights. They grew exponentially, miniature beams that, as Annie lowered, revealed themselves to be the eyes of children, splashing in the Shoot-the-Chutes, spinning in the Tilt-A-Whirl, riding every carousel horse, laughing and playing. There had to be thousands of them.

"I worked here my whole life," Eddie yelled from their midst. "Keeping rides safe meant keeping kids safe. And because they were safe, they grew up and had kids of their own. And their kids had kids, and their kids will have kids."

He motioned to the sea of young faces. "My heaven lets me see them all."

Annie's cart lowered to the platform.

"Do you understand what I'm saying?"

"I'm not sure," Annie replied.

Eddie turned away.

"Because I saved you, as tough as those years were for you, as bad as it was with your hand, you got to grow up, too. And because you got to grow up . . ."

When he turned back, Annie froze. Eddie was holding a baby boy, with a small blue cap on his head.

"Laurence?" Annie whispered.

Eddie stepped forward and placed her son in her trembling arms. Instantly, Annie was whole again, her body complete. She cradled the infant against her chest, a motherly cradle that filled her with the purest feeling. She smiled and she wept and she could not stop weeping.

"My baby," she gushed. "Oh, my baby, my baby . . ."

She wiggled his toes. She tickled his little fingers. Her tears dripped onto his tiny forehead and he swatted them away, eyes dancing with alertness. It was clear that somehow, he knew Annie, as Annie knew him back. Her son existed. He was safe here in heaven. Annie felt a serenity that mortal life had never allowed.

"Thank you," she whispered to Eddie.

Before he could reply, she was whisked into the sky, away from the amusement park and past the single bright star of Tala, into the dead, black vacuum of another universe. When Annie looked down, she saw her arms were empty, and she howled in anguish, feeling utterly full and utterly vacant, which is what having and losing a child is like.

SUNDAY, **3**:o7 P.M.

As the police car approached the hospital, Tolbert looked out the window at the long streaks of clouds. He said a silent prayer. This, he knew, would be the last moment hope could overshadow fact. Once he got inside, whatever he saw would be undeniable.

The car stopped. He took a deep breath, then opened the door, tugged on his jacket, stepped out quickly, and walked beside the policeman. Neither man spoke.

They entered through the emergency entrance. As they approached the desk, Tolbert spotted, through a side curtain, his assistant, Teddy, sitting on the edge of a gurney, with his head down and his hands over his ears.

For an instant, Tolbert felt relief. *He's alive. Thank God.* Then came rage. He stormed through the opening.

"Whoa, hey—" the officer said. But Tolbert grabbed Teddy by the shoulders and yelled, "What the hell, Teddy? What the hell?"

Teddy's mouth was an oval. His body trembled.

"Wind," he muttered. "An electrical line. I tried to avoid—"

"Did you check the damn weather?"

"I—"

"Did you check the damn weather?"

"It was—"

"Why did you go up? Who were these people? What the hell, Teddy?"

The police officer pulled Tolbert back, saying, "Easy, pal, easy." Gasping for breath, Teddy pulled a business card from his shirt pocket.

"They said they *knew* you," he croaked.

Tolbert froze. The card was frayed, as if it had been rained on. Tolbert's name was handwritten on the back.

"Excuse me, are you the balloon owner?"

Tolbert spun. Another officer was in front of him.

"We need to get a statement."

Tolbert swallowed. "Why?"

The officer flipped open a notepad.

"There's a fatality," he said.

The Final Eternity

Annie slumped on a cold, hard surface, her soul torn in half. She had held her baby. She had felt at peace. For one blessed moment, she thought she had found her eternal rest. She would live forever in the starry sunshine of Ruby Pier, with her son, Laurence, with Eddie, the old man, with the other children he had kept alive. That would be her heaven.

But she was gone from that heaven now, and it was clear there was no going back. She felt gutted. Hollowed out. She lacked the will to even open her eyes. When she did, no colors moved across the firmament. Blackness draped as if the air were opaque.

Why go on? she thought, slumping back. Her life had been revealed by the people she'd met, and her deepest secrets had been ripped open, abandoned by the sentinels her brain had once sent to protect them.

She knew everything that had happened now.

She knew why others had been involved. What she did not know was how it all fit together, or, most agonizingly, how her life had ended. *Is this it?* she thought. The sum of her existence? A cut cord, loose and dangling?

As a child, Annie had been taught that when she died, the Lord would take her in and all would be comfort and peace. Perhaps that was meant for those with completed missions. If you didn't finish your story on earth, how could heaven do it for you?

She ran her hands around her body and winced. Her head hurt, her shoulders were sore, and her lower back was tight, recalling the pain after she fell from the balloon. When she pushed her palms towards her thighs, she felt a familiar fabric, soft and satiny, and as she pushed lower, it widened and frilled.

She knew, without seeing, that she was back in her wedding dress.

☙

Get up, she heard her inner voice tell her. *Finish this.* Weak and dazed, Annie rose in the darkness. Her feet were bare. The dress clung to her body. Looking down, she saw specks of light through the clear surface. Stars. First a few, then thousands, a galaxy's worth, all below her heels.

She took a step.

The ground rolled.

Annie stopped.

It stopped as well.

She took another step and it rolled with her; she was walking atop some sort of globe—a massive glass globe with an entire universe inside it. At another time, it might have interested her. But she was blank now, a shelled husk. She trudged ahead with no peace, no clarity, none of the "salvation" that had enlightened Eddie.

Just when she imagined this was her permanent fate, she began to pass objects scattered here and there: a beige lawn chair lying on its side, a music stand turned upside down, white ribbons that were cut between two metal stanchions. A new feeling overtook her, raw and unsettling, a feeling that this was less someone else's heaven than the remains of her earth.

Up ahead, she saw a canopy. Under the canopy, she saw the backs of several people, men and women, in suits and bridesmaid dresses.

"Hello?" she yelled.

Silence.

"Can you hear me?"

Nothing.

"Please, someone, tell me where I am," she pleaded, drawing closer. "Do any of you know me?"

The figures dissolved into tiny particles, revealing a single tuxedoed man who lifted his head.

"I do," Paulo said.

The Fifth Person Annie Meets in Heaven

Love comes when you least expect it. Love comes when you most need it. Love comes when you are ready to receive it or can no longer deny it. These are common expressions that hold varying truths of love. But the truth of love for Annie was that, for a long time, nearly ten years, she expected none and got none in return.

After the loss of her mother and her child, Annie withdrew from almost everyone, burying herself in her nursing routine. She dressed the same each day: blue scrubs and gray running shoes. She drove the same roads through town. She purchased the same cup of tea at the same café.

And day after day, she tended to her patients. She kept their charts. She knew their doctors. She avoided working in pediatrics, finding the memories too difficult. But she was quite good with the elderly; she encouraged their conversation, and they were happy to prattle on. Annie discovered listening to older patients was a form of medicine—for them and for her. It was just enough caring, but not enough to hurt her. And not being hurt was now the driving force in Annie's life.

She took extra shifts. She let work fill her days and nights. She rarely socialized. She didn't date. She pulled her butterscotch curls into a small black elastic and turned the light off in her heart.

Then came the morning when, walking to the hospital, her tea lukewarm and nearly finished, she glanced up and felt everything flip, because there, on a platform, was Paulo, grown-up Paulo, wearing faded blue jeans and hammering a board. A lever pulled in the basement of her soul, and Annie's blood coursed and her nerve endings tingled.

Don't look at me, she thought. *I can still get away if you don't—*

"Hey, I know you," he said, a grin rising. "You're Annie!"

She slid her left hand behind her.

"That's me, all right."

"From school."

"From school."

"I'm Paulo."

"I remember."

"From school."

"From school."

"Wow. Annie."

She felt her skin flush. She could not fathom why a boy from high school should have such an effect on her now. But when he said, "Wow. Annie," she could not help but think the same thing: *Wow. Annie. What is this?*

And while she didn't know it then, she was learning another truth about love: it comes when it comes.

Simple as that.

Their romance was less a courtship than a reunion. They had dinner that night and every night that week. They laughed and talked, late and long, avoiding early awkwardness thanks to their shared childhood.

Paulo told lots of stories, and when he finished one, Annie, chin in hand, would ask, "Then what?" He'd had many adventures once his family moved to Italy, with villagers, horsemen, a traveling soccer team, a year in the mountains that turned dangerous. Annie felt as if these tales had been saved up just for her.

"What about you?" Paulo asked. "How is your mom?"

"She died."

"I'm sorry."

"Yeah."

"I liked her, Annie."

"But she chased you away."

"She was fierce. She wanted to protect you." Paulo shrugged. "That's *why* I liked her."

They hugged briefly that first night together, patting each other's backs like old friends. But a few nights later, after a spaghetti dinner, they kissed gently in the front of Paulo's car. Annie pulled back as if it were the only time she had ever kissed anyone. She told Paulo she'd been holding that kiss since the day he left high school—"I'm not counting that disaster at your locker"—and Paulo said he'd felt awful about that incident and the way those kids had acted, the way he had acted, too.

"That Megan was a witch," Annie said.

"But your drawing was cool. Do you still have it?"

Annie burst out laughing. "Do I still *have* it?"

"Yeah."

"Why?"

"Because I want it."

"You want the drawing?"

"Of course. That drawing was how I knew you loved me."

Annie looked down, rubbing her knee.

"You didn't know that," she said, softly.

"Sure, I did. I knew I loved *you*."

She lifted her gaze. "Are you joking?"

"No way."

"Then why didn't you say something?"

"Annie," Paulo said, that big grin widening, "I was fourteen!"

In time, as with the truest loves, their lives melded seamlessly, and they knew it would stay that way without ever saying a word.

One day, during a lunch break, Annie wheeled a patient named Mrs. Velichek into the new seniors wing. She was from New York and had just passed her ninetieth birthday, frail in body but brimming with spirit. Annie liked her.

"What do you think?" Annie asked. "It's bigger than the old—"

She stopped. There, kneeling on the floor, was Paulo, finishing the molding. He looked up.

"Good morning, beautiful."

"He's not talking to *me*," Mrs. Velichek said.

"How do you know?" Annie said.

"Yeah, how do you know?" Paulo added, rising to shake the woman's hand.

"Mrs. Velichek, this is Paulo. We're friends," Annie said.

Paulo nodded towards the counter. "It looks like the food's here."

Annie saw loaves of bread and assorted cold cuts that someone had delivered.

"That's not for us," she said.

"It's not *not* for us," Paulo said, mischievously. "Are you hungry, Mrs. Velichek?"

A minute later, Paulo and Annie were playfully making sandwiches. Paulo stuffed them high with meat.

"Not so big," Annie cautioned.

"Don't listen to her!" Mrs. Velichek said.

"I always listen to her," Paulo said.

"He *better*," Annie replied, but she laughed and elbowed Paulo when she said it.

"Friends, huh?" Mrs. Velichek said. "Honey, who are you kidding?"

⁓

They moved in together a month later, and their routines intertwined, like paint colors fading into each other. They shared breakfast, shared toothpaste, shared a cold, shared a mailing address.

Autumn came and winter came and spring came and melted into summer. One bright morning, before leaving for work, Paulo pulled the elastic out of Annie's hair and she shook free her wavy locks. "Better?" she said, and he said, "Better," and they could have been talking about everything.

Their marriage was a formality after that. But Paulo had a showman's heart. He waited until one night, when he had things ready, and he led Annie to the roof of their building, which was lit by small torches and serenaded by classical music from a large white speaker. He pulled a sheet off a large lumpy shape to reveal an unusual sculpture: two giant papier-mâché frogs. He had made them to mark the day they met in the schoolyard. One frog wore a necktie and was leaping over the other. Attached to the necktie was a note.

Annie read it.

"One small step for frog, one giant leap for the two of us?"

She burst out laughing. As she turned to Paulo, he already had a ring box open, and Annie didn't even wait to hear the question.

"Yes," she gushed. "Yes. Yes. Yes."

∽

"No," Annie whispered now.

Paulo blinked.

"You can't be here."

He opened his hands.

"I don't want you to be here!"

He reached for her cheek.

"Don't touch me! Don't be here! You had to live! You had to live!"

His fingers grazed her skin, and her entire body seemed to melt with the contact.

"Look, Annie," he said, "the northern lights."

Beneath them, through the glassy surface, waves of green and red moved like smoke through the stars.

"Do you know what causes them?"

Annie felt tears streaming down her face.

"You told me so many times," she answered, her voice quivering. "Particles fly off the sun. They blow to earth on solar winds. They take two days to reach us. And they break into our atmosphere . . ."

She choked up.

"At the top of the world."

"And here we are," Paulo said.

He waved his hand and a magnificent wash of colors swept the sky beneath their feet. Annie stared at her husband, who looked the way he'd looked at their wedding, but so at peace, his eyes creaseless, his lips without a single line. There was no one she wanted to see more. There was no one she wanted to see less.

"*Why?*" she whispered. "Why are you here?"

"The winds blew," he said.

The Fifth Lesson

Loss is as old as life itself. But for all our evolution, we are yet to accept it.

Annie, realizing she had not saved Paulo's life, felt consumed by her losses now. From the father who left early, to the hand damaged by the accident, to the home she was forced to leave, to the friends she left behind, to her mother's death, to her lost child, to her wedding night, to this, her husband, here in front of her. Her final loss.

She had failed again.

"How long have you been here?" she asked.

"A little while."

"Will you meet five people?"

"I already have."

"I don't understand. Did I die after you?"

"Time is different here, Annie. A few seconds on

earth could be a century in heaven. It's wild. Better than all my nerdy space books."

He smiled, and Annie felt the corners of her own mouth rising. But then she remembered where they were.

"No," she insisted. "It's not fair. We had one night being married."

"One night can change a lot."

"It's not enough!" She looked at him like a pleading child. "I don't understand, Paulo. Why couldn't we just be happy? Why was everything good taken away from me?"

Paulo gazed at the black firmament as if checking something, even though there was nothing there.

"Remember that last day in high school?" he said. "I actually ran after you. I saw you in the park. You were crying on a bench, but I couldn't bring myself to talk to you. I knew that I'd let you down.

"We moved the next day, and for fifteen years, that gnawed at me. As young as we were, I felt I'd lost someone important, someone precious. I came home to America hoping one day to see you again. Then, out of the blue, there you were, at the hospital. And I realized, if you truly love someone, you'll find a way back."

Annie frowned. "And then you lose them again."

"You lose something every day you live, Annie. Sometimes it's as tiny as the breath you just expelled, sometimes it's so big you think you won't survive it."

He took her left hand. "But you do, right?"

Annie felt an arterial burst of love. Her husband was here. At least she could be with him. And yet . . .

"I wanted to save you," she whispered.

"You gave me a lung."

"But you still *died*."

"That doesn't change what you did."

"How are you so at peace with this? All I feel is . . ."

"What?"

Annie searched for the word. "Heartbroken."

Paulo thought for a moment. "I want to show you something."

He reached inside his jacket pocket and removed a pipe cleaner rabbit.

"You gave me that already," Annie said.

"Watch."

Suddenly, the rabbit untwisted magically into five straightened pipe cleaners. Paulo took one and made a simple double-humped shape.

"This is the heart we're born with, Annie. It's small and empty because it's been through nothing."

He put it in her hand.

"And this . . ."

He took the four other pipe cleaners and twisted them to create a larger, complicated version, with lines crisscrossing the insides.

"This is the heart we die with. After the people we love. After all our losses. It's bigger, you see?"

"But it's broken," Annie said.

"Yes."

"That's what ruins it."

Paulo pushed the heart to Annie's chest.

"No. That's what makes it whole."

Suddenly, the pipe cleaners glowed brilliantly and Annie felt a small thumping growing inside her.

"Paulo, what's happening?"

"Thank you, Annie. For a minute, I got to breathe as you. It was amazing."

"No, wait—"

"You have to go now."

"I want to be with *you*—"

"I'll be right here. But for now, you have to live."

"Live?"

"You were saved from dying once, Annie. You owe the world some saving in return. It's why you became a nurse. And why you need to go back. To save someone else."

"No, Paulo. Please!"

He let go of her hand. Annie saw pieces of herself disappearing, first her feet and arms, then her knees, thighs, belly, chest, decomposing all that she had reconstructed during the afterlife. The surface beneath her seemed to flatten and melt, and she heard two levels of sounds, as if multiple tapes were playing at once. Paulo was fading into the brilliant glow of the northern lights. Only his face was visible now, close enough to touch. He kissed her, softly, and she tried desperately to hold on to him, to lock him in her gaze, but her lids drooped like heavy curtains and everything went dark. Then Annie felt his two hands on her shoulders, pushing her from heaven to earth.

She knew those hands had been there before.

"See you in a little bit," Paulo whispered.

When her eyes opened, Annie was staring into a fluorescent ceiling light. She heard a soft mechanical humming and a woman's voice say, "Doctor, look!"

Epilogue

News of the balloon crash spread quickly through the state and in time reached even the farthest corners of the world. People shared photos and made comments on the frailty of life.

The story told was of a newlywed couple, an inexperienced pilot, and a lucky ending for two of the three passengers. The pilot, who flew the balloon into an electrical line, escaped death by tumbling out of the basket. The bride was thrown to safety by her brave husband, who then jumped to earth and, despite massive injuries, survived for hours, including several minutes after receiving a lung from his wife. He expired in the operating room at the same moment she slipped into a coma due to complications from the transplant.

What few people knew was that the doctors, briefly, lost Annie as well. She flatlined in her co-

matose state before being revived by a team that included her Uncle Dennis, who burst into tears when
her heart began to beat again.

"You're OK now, Annie. You're gonna be OK."

He forced a smile. "You gave us a scare."

Annie blinked.

For the first time in a long time, she didn't feel
scared at all.

Time passed. Like flakes shaken in a snow globe, the
lives of those involved in the tragedy settled slowly
to the ground, not in the same spots but in new
pockets of peace.

Teddy moved to another state, joined a church,
and spent much of his time leading discussions about
second chances. Tolbert closed his business and sold
the property. He spent five months summoning the
courage to write the widowed bride. A week later,
he got a letter back.

At her request, Tolbert drove to Annie's home
and was stunned to see her answer the door, visi-
bly pregnant. She was kinder than he expected and
seemed remarkably calm in light of all that had happened. Tolbert told Annie repeatedly how sorry he
was, how much he liked Paulo from their brief en-

counter in the rain. Before he left, he asked if Annie could ever forgive him for the events that led to her husband's death, but she insisted that wasn't necessary.

"Winds blew," she said.

Tolbert left, never knowing another wind that had blown, one he had diverted, yanking Paulo to the side of the road on that rainy night, preventing a speeding car from striking him, a tragedy that a different version of the world had planned, a version that did not grant Annie and Paulo even one night of marriage, nor the child that would come from it. But there are so many times our lives are altered invisibly. The flip of a pencil, from written to erased.

Shortly after that visit, Annie got a map, packed a small bag, and made a journey in her car to an amusement park by a great gray ocean. Upon reaching the entrance, she stepped out and stared at the spires and minarets of Ruby Pier, the bejeweled front arch and a tower drop ride that hovered above it all.

She asked staff members if there was anyone who remembered a man named Eddie, who used to fix the rides. She was taken to a maintenance shop behind the bumper car ride, a shop with low ceilings and dim bulbs and porcelain clown heads and coffee cans full of screws and bolts. Annie was introduced to a middle-aged man named Dominguez, who wiped his hands on a rag and said yes, he used to work for Eddie, right up to his death. When Annie told him who she was, he dropped the rag and slumped back on a stool, nearly toppling over.

For a moment, he could only mumble, "Oh, man. Oh, man."

Then he began to cry.

"I'm sorry. It's just . . . Eddie would be so happy if he knew you were OK."

Annie smiled.

Later, Dominguez took her to the back and showed her a chest of Eddie's possessions, knick-knacks and birthday cards and a pair of army boots. Annie asked if she could take a box of pipe cleaners. Dominguez said if she wanted, she could have the whole chest.

"Can I ask you something personal?" he said before they parted.

Annie nodded.

"How does it feel to have your life saved? I mean, I saw what happened that day at the park. If not for Eddie, you would have died."

Annie touched her belly. She said it was hard to explain. She said she used to feel that she'd give anything to change what had happened, but now she felt differently. Mostly, she said, she felt grateful.

Seasons came and seasons went, and when the days grew hot, the crowds returned to the seaside amusement parks, and kids rode the newest version of the tower drop ride at Ruby Pier, unaware, as children blessedly are, of previous fates that were altered in its space.

Annie, meanwhile, gave birth to a daughter, whom she cradled gently to her chest. She called her Giovanna, an Italian name for "gift from God," because, as Paulo had suggested, Annie returned from heaven to bring her into the world.

One day, when Giovanna was four years old, Annie took her outside to look at the stars.

"They're so high, Mommy!"

"Yes, they are."

"Is there anything higher?"

Annie only grinned. She never spoke about her journey through the afterlife, not to anyone. But she did not intend to be silent forever.

One day, when Giovanna was old enough, Annie would tell her a story about heaven. She would tell her of the people who were already there, her Grandma and her older brother and her Daddy in a tuxedo, watching the stars. She would tell her of the secrets she had learned on her visit, how one life touches another and that life touches the next.

She would tell her that all endings are also beginnings, we just don't know it at the time. And for the rest of her days, the child would be comforted knowing whatever her fears or losses, heaven held the answers to all her earthly questions, beginning with five people who were waiting for her, as they wait for us all, under the eyes of God and in the true meaning of that most precious word.

Home.

To my cherished readers,

This book was dedicated to a certain little girl.

My next book will be about her.

Happily, unlike Annie, this little girl was real. Sadly, unlike Annie, her journey to heaven was not temporary.

Her name was Chika Jeune, a beautiful, brave and curious Haitian child, who was born three days before the horrific earthquake of 2010 and who survived it by a miracle.

The story of how she came to an orphanage I operate in Port Au Prince, then was diagnosed with an operable brain tumor at age five, then came to live with my wife and me in America for two years as we tried desperately to save her, is, to this stage, the biggest story of my life.

So after hesitating, ruminating, smiling, and crying over it, I've decided to share that story, and all the laughter, love, and illumination that having Chika as our little girl brought us.

If you enjoyed *The Next Person You Meet in Heaven*, I hope you will consider reading *Finding*

Chika, as many of the themes developed in these pages came from the things she showed me.

The Next Person is about the mistakes we think we make, and how they are part of what connects us to the human core.

Finding Chika is about how those same connections allow us, at any age, even with the most unlikely pairings, to make a family.

Becoming a de facto father was an indelible, joyous experience. And with grace, I plan to create a joyous book, one I hope we can share.

Thank you, as always, for taking my stories into your hearts and minds.

Most sincerely,
Mitch Albom

Acknowledgments

The author would first like to thank God for the blessings of health and creativity that allow a man to create a story about heaven in the first place.

In addition, many thanks to the following people for help and inspiration in creating this book:

First, from the research areas: Kay MacConnachie, occupational therapist and clinical manager at Motus Rehabilitation in Warren, Michigan, whose work with patients recovering from hand replantation helped paint a vivid portrait of the emotional and physical scars that followed Annie her entire life; Gordon Boring, hot air balloon pilot and president of Wicker Basket Balloon Center in Wixom, Michigan (and, readers: please know, accidents like the one described here are extraordinarily rare!); Lisa Allenspach, senior staff physician at Henry Ford Hospital and medical director of the

Henry Ford Hospital Lung Transplant Program in Detroit; and Val Gokenbach, chief nursing officer at Baylor Scott & White All Saints Medical Center–Fort Worth, in Texas. Special thanks to Jo-Ann Barnas, who did meticulous research and asked great questions. And the character of Sameer was inspired in part by the true story of the late Everett (Eddie) Knowles, whose accident as a child in 1962 led to a breakthrough in the field of limb reattachment.

In addition, the author wishes to thank David Black, an agent and friend through thick and thin; Gary Morris, Jennifer Herrera, and Matt Belford of the David Black Agency; and the great folks at HarperCollins, starting with Karen Rinaldi, my cherished editor and publisher, who gave me great insight into female protagonists; Jonathan Burnham; Brian Murray; Hannah Robinson; Doug Jones; Frank Albanese; Leah Wasielewski; Stephanie Cooper; Sarah Lambert; Tina Andreadis; Leslie Cohen; Leah Carlson-Stanisic; Michael Siebert; and Milan Bozic (who gave us another amazing cover).

On the home front, many thanks to Kerri Alexander, who keeps my life straight, and Marc "Rosey" Rosenthal, who keeps that life from falling apart; to Vince and Frank; to Antonella Iannarino, our amazing web guru; and to Mendel, who is still a bum.

There would be no Five People concept without my Uncle Eddie—the real Eddie—who told me my first story of the afterlife. And when the fictional Eddie says it wouldn't be heaven without his wife, that was me talking about Janine, who inspires me every day; to my family members who gave this book its early reads; and to my mother and father, who taught me how to tell stories and who have, since my last book, joined each other in heaven, where they no doubt are spending every minute together, as they tried to do on earth.

Finally, my deepest thanks to my readers, who continue to surprise me, inspire me, motivate me, and bless me. For now, heaven may be a prayer and a guess. But I know, thanks to you, I have experienced some of it already.